The Magician's Curse
The Great Dagmaru
Book 1

Linda G. Hill

This is a work of fiction. Names, characters, places, and incidents either are the products of the author's imagination or are used fictitiously. Any resemblance to actual persons, living or dead, organizations, events, or locales is entirely coincidental.

THE MAGICIAN'S CURSE – THE GREAT DAGMARU, BOOK 1

Cover: "Fetus" by Belinda Borradaile

For information, visit https://lindaghill.com

ISBN: (print) 978-0-9948912-2-8
ISBN: (e-book) 978-0-9948912-1-1

FIRST EDITION

For Darren, who was there at the beginning

Prologue

Tarmien Dagmar couldn't sleep. The clock taunted him as it had for months, even before his first child was born.

At least Stella can rest, he thought, listening to the soft snores of his wife drift through the dark from the other side of their king-sized bed. Breastfeeding was taking its toll, but the mere mention of hiring a nanny or allowing the servants to help with diaper changes was met with a firm "no."

Murmuring something incoherent, she rolled over to face him and his blood heated at the fleeting thought of impregnating her again. It was what he was made for, after all. The blood that coursed through his veins, handed down for centuries from father to son, contained that of a demon. An incubus. A creature whose sole purpose was to seduce women and to create offspring.

Tarmien was coaxed from his thoughts by the subtle but distinctive sound of a waking infant. He gently eased himself out of bed so as not to wake his wife and crossed the hall quickly.

"It's okay, Stephen," he whispered as he closed the door of the nursery behind him. "Daddy's here."

He reached into the crib and picked up the restless newborn who settled the moment he was cradled in his father's arms.

What have I done? Tarmien asked himself for the thousandth time since the baby was born.

Apart from the insatiable desire to procreate, Tarmien hadn't shown any of the demonic tendencies to which his father had confessed on his deathbed, just months ago. He hoped he could spare his son the knowledge of that horrible confession. At least the curse that tied the Dagmar family to their servants, the Currys, was a burden Tarmien could bear himself; he was determined this child would never have to carry out its twisted conditions.

As he lifted his precious son to kiss his fine, black hair and breathe in his potent baby scent, he prayed that the family's demonic bloodline had run out, once and for all. Only time would tell.

.

Chapter 1

Things don't always go as planned. Herman Anderson had almost eighteen years of hard-earned experience with this. What she hadn't yet learned was how much it could be true. Her first taste of plans going awry on this, the first day back to school after March Break, came with her brother, Chad, missing his school bus.

"You have everything now?" They stood in the mudroom at the back door of their parents' house. She kept her voice down so she wouldn't wake their mother.

"Wait," he said.

She squeezed her eyes shut and held in a scream of frustration while he checked the contents of his enormous green gym bag one more time. It hadn't taken her as long to stuff everything she owned into her backpack that morning as it took the obsessive-compulsive eleven-year-old to leave home for the day. And he'd had a whole week to get ready.

"Yeah, I think so," he said, hefting his bag onto his shoulder.

"If I wasn't so worried about you, I'd kill you right now."

Chad grimaced. "I'll be okay. It'll just be a few days, right?"

"As long as Dad comes home to look after you and Mom, which he should. Otherwise, I'll come back and get you as soon as school's finished in June." She eyed the umbrella he'd plucked out of the corner. "You're not taking that on my bike. You'll probably end up impaling us both." She graced him with the evilest eye she could muster and he dropped the umbrella.

"Thank you. Let's go."

Outside in the warmish humidity—a relief after a cold Ottawa winter—she mounted her bicycle with Chad on the back and rode with the kind of energy few possessed quite like a healthy teenage girl who had been cooped up inside for months. She was ready to move on, more than anything else she'd ever been ready for in her life. Chad was prepared, Herman mused as she skirted puddles, runoff from the rapidly melting snow banks. She wouldn't be leaving at all if she wasn't convinced of this.

Fifteen minutes later she stopped in front of Chad's school. The absence of children's voices on the playground whispered, "You're late," but she resolved to take all the time she needed to make sure he was going to be okay.

"If you're desperate for anything, tell Jason's mom." Jason was Chad's best friend. "And you know where the money is so you can buy food if you need it?"

"In the box on the top shelf of your closet."

"And don't tell anyone where I've gone. Especially Dad."

"*I* don't know where you're going."

"And stay out of trouble at school. I don't want them calling Mom. You know what to tell her if she asks where I've gone?"

"That you're staying at a friend's place. If she even notices you're missing."

"You've got the emergency number for Dad?"

Chad patted his jacket pocket. "One copy here, one at home in the cookie jar. I'll call him after school today."

"And you know what to say?"

He cocked his head to the side and spoke tiredly, as though he'd repeated it a thousand times already. "'Herman's gone, she left a note, the note says she won't be back, blah, blah, blah.'"

She pinched her brother's nose. "You gonna be okay, Squirt?"

"Yeah, and don't call me 'Squirt.'"

Herman sighed. "Fine. You've got the key to my bike lock?"

"Yep. I'll pick it up at the train station on the weekend. By that time, Dad should be able to drive me to get it."

"I'd have left it at home and taken the bus if you hadn't been late this morning."

Guilt struck her in the stomach when Chad looked down at his shoes.

"This is really it. One-way trip."

"I'll be back. Hug?"

Her brother embraced her and turned to go, walking away in his jeans and bomber jacket, every bit like the typical kid he was. "Get lost before you miss your train," he called over his shoulder.

She couldn't bear to look back.

Another fifteen minutes later, Herman stepped aboard a VIA Rail car with half a minute to spare. She shuffled down the aisle and plopped herself into a window seat. Looking through the glass, she watched a fine rain begin to fall as she pushed away her misgivings at leaving her brother behind. If all went well, her new live-in position on a thoroughbred horse farm—a dream job, in Herman's opinion—would be secure, and then she could ask if Chad could come and live with her. She didn't think she would have any problems getting him away from her parents. Their dad, George Anderson of the great unknown job that took him away for months at a time, had to be forced to come home. Herman had come to the conclusion that nothing would make that happen short of her leaving. Their mother was barely well enough to look after herself, let alone her kids, and her decline was beginning to scare Herman.

A young, preppy blond guy in a beige blazer and turtleneck to match, who probably had a name that ended in "The Third," slid into the seat beside her. He smelled heavily of Old Spice, reminding her of her father when she was little.

"Off on an adventure too?" he asked, eying her backpack. All he lacked was a British accent.

Herman shrugged.

"I certainly am. Leaving home. I've had enough of all that utter codswallop."

She nodded and returned to watching the rain dot the window. Just a couple of runaways.

"I can't believe they expect me to live under their thumb. Curfews. *Pfft.*"

Herman turned to the young man. "I know, right? Looking after a disabled mom and a little brother, having to wonder if my dad's going to come home this month and how drunk he'll be when he does. Bullshit, right? You thinking about changing your name, too?"

"Well, it's not quite …"

"That bad? No, I didn't think so."

Herman turned and put her forehead to the glass. Thankfully Mr. The Third disembarked in Brockville without another word. That was when the man who would change the remainder of her plans boarded the train.

Compared to the stifling soul who had previously occupied the seat beside Herman, he was a breath of fresh air, quite literally. The shoulders of his trench coat, wet from the rain, smelled of spring and his damp hair hung in a raven sheen to his shoulders.

She gawked at his profile, mannequin-like in its perfection but for a slight bump on the bridge of his nose. He settled a leather bag between his feet on the floor and then rummaged through his coat pockets for something he seemed to have misplaced. His coat, like his hair, his bag, and everything else that adorned him, was black. Herman realized she was staring. She'd seen the kind of beautiful people whose faces kept drawing her back for a glance, but she'd never been so close to one before.

With her pulse pounding in her throat, she asked, "Lost something?"

For the first time in her life, Herman saw someone do a genuine double take and she suppressed a smile.

"My keys." He frowned, his keys seemingly forgotten. "Have we met before?" One exquisite eyebrow rose a fraction.

"No. Not at all."

Stupid thing to say, she admonished herself, attempting, but failing, to drag her gaze away from his face.

His features were symmetrical until he grinned. His full upper lip rose slightly more on the right. "In that case, I'm Stephen." He held out his hand.

"I'm Herman," she said, clasping it. Her plan to change her name went out the window without a thought. He was warm to the touch, and he squeezed her hand just right. His irises were dark mahogany with a reddish tinge, the only color about him other than black and his flawless, pale skin.

"I'm sorry," he said, stealing his hand from her grasp. "I'm being impolite, staring at you."

Herman laughed nervously. "I seem to be doing the same thing." She reluctantly turned to the window. In the reflection, she saw that his body was still angled in her direction. Comparing her own image to his was like dull brown cotton to luxurious satin. It came to her belatedly that he didn't flinch at her unusual name. Another first.

She was relieved to have a reason to look at him again when he spoke. "I can't get over the idea that you look familiar, somehow." He gazed into her eyes and she into his. Her face heated and she glanced away again. Where had her earlier coolness gone?

"I'm making you uncomfortable. I should leave you alone."

"No!" She snapped her head back and touched his sleeve. His eyes shifted to her hand and she jerked it away.

"I'm sorry. I'm usually better at talking to strangers."

"Normally, I am too." He smiled and it was as though the heavens had opened up and dropped an angel beside her. She felt her eyes widen and her lips part but she was powerless to prevent it. "But today," he continued, "I seem to be at a loss. I hope to get a few intelligible sentences out of my mouth before I get to Kingston, though."

"Are you only going as far as Kingston?" She was full of clever comments.

"Yes. Are you going to Toronto? Or ..."

"Yeah, I'm going to Toronto," she said, filled with sudden regret. She put her hand over the hole in her jeans, hoping beyond hope that the rip looked designer.

He glanced down at the movement and back up to her eyes. "Are you visiting family there?"

"No, I'm supposed to be starting a new job."

"That's exciting."

"I guess." She shrugged. It *had* been exciting until a few minutes ago.

"What will you be doing, if you don't mind my asking?"

"Mucking out stalls at a horse farm north of the city. Really glamorous stuff. It's a live-in position."

"Do you like horses?"

"Yeah," she said unenthusiastically.

"I do too. I have horses at home. I use them in my work sometimes."

"Really?"

"Yes." He folded his hands in his lap and leaned back. "I have to admit, I'm disappointed that you already have employment to go to."

"I'm not too attached to it," she said, aghast at herself. "Why do you say that?"

"Well, I'm looking for an assistant." He smiled again and her stomach twisted into a knot of unparalleled excitement.

The overwhelming sensation that it was too good to be true filled her head. Not only was she talking to the most gorgeous man she'd ever seen, but he was offering her a job? It would have to be magic.

"What kind of assistant do you need?" she managed to ask.

"I'm a magician."

She barked out a laugh.

"What is it?" His eyes were warmly curious.

"Oh, just that I was thinking this must be magic and you happen to be ..." she laughed again, and he laughed with her.

"It does kind of seem magic, doesn't it?" He licked his lips and she dropped her gaze from his face. It was impossible to look at him and not feel like she was gawking.

He bent his head to get her attention. "This may sound really weird, and I don't want to make you uncomfortable, but I feel as though we were supposed to meet today, on this train." He smiled lopsidedly and shook his head. "No, I shouldn't have said that. It sounds too strange."

"No," Herman said, "I agree. Or at least I'd like to think it was some kind of destiny thing." She laughed. "You're right. It's weird when you actually say it."

"It is. So, about the position—I hate to ask you to drop what you were doing, but I feel this might be my only chance. Are you interested?"

"I—"

"Wait," he interrupted. "How old are you? I'm not sure if I can even ask you to get off the train with me, without breaking a law."

"I'll be eighteen in three weeks," Herman said. "How old are you?" She blushed, realizing she'd asked him a personal question that had more to do with the desire to be in his arms than work for him.

"I'm twenty-three. Which is why I can't ask you to get off the train with me, unfortunately."

She thought about it for the space of a breath, gathered up what was left of her sanity, and put it aside. "What if I said I wanted to get off the train with you?"

"Then I'd ask how soon would you like to start?"

Her head swam. It was work, which was what she was after, but … "As your assistant. Does that mean onstage? I don't know the first thing about magic," she said, instantly regretting her words.

"You don't have to. I can teach you everything you need to know. And you'll have a place to stay in my guest room, so you don't have to worry about that. I'll be working from home—there's plenty of room there for you—until I go on the road, and then we'll stay in hotels. With separate rooms, of course."

Too bad, she thought, feeling her face go red again. There *had* to be a catch. "But why?" she asked. "Why me?"

He dropped his gaze. Then, looking up, he said, "Would you believe that now I've found you, I can't bear to say goodbye to you?"

"I probably wouldn't if I didn't feel the same way. But I don't know if I can get over the feeling this is all too good to be true."

He pulled his cell phone from his pocket and checked the time. "We'll be in Kingston in twenty minutes, so you have a little while to decide."

Twenty minutes to make what might be the stupidest decision of my life, Herman thought. Yet it felt like the decision was already made, somehow. There was an energy about him, a mystical force that drew her in.

He offered her the phone. "Would you be more comfortable if you called your family to let them know?"

"No," she said, raising her hand to ward it off. "I don't need to call anyone."

"I have an idea." He held up one finger and leaned forward, shifting his long, leather-clad legs to rummage through his bag.

He laughed. "My keys!" he said, dangling them in the air. "See? I can conjure things out of nowhere."

Herman giggled. "I'm glad you found them."

"But that's not what I was looking for." When he finally sat back, he had a sheet of paper in his hand.

"This is one of my promotional posters," he said, handing it to her. It was a picture of him in profile, wearing a tux and top hat, holding a ball of light up to the level of his forehead. The poster said that he, The Great Dagmaru, would be putting on a show in Miami, Florida, on the 27th of November last year. In the photograph, he was almost as beautiful as he was in real life, sitting beside her, watching her.

"Nice picture. The Great Dagma*roo*?"

"Dag-ma-ru. No emphasis on any of the syllables. I adopted the name a while ago, and it stuck. My last name is Dagmar."

"Ah." Was this, after all, any worse than the unseen job she was already going to? The phrase "the devil you know versus the devil you don't" came to mind. This devil she knew, relatively speaking, and he almost certainly looked better than the elderly-sounding one she had spoken to on the phone. And he seemed legitimate.

"Why don't I come home with you then, and we'll go from there? If that's okay." She shook her head. "I can't believe I just said that. Going home with a stranger I just met on a train. Every parent's worst nightmare and I'm it."

"I can assure you I'm not a bad guy. I'm only a

magician."

He pulled a blue paper flower out of thin air and offered it to her, making her laugh.

"Can you make it disappear?"

"I can," he said with a grin. "But I'd rather you kept it."

She took the flower. "Will you make me disappear?"

"Not from where you can't be reached. Any time you want to, you'll be free to contact anyone you'd like."

She nodded. "Do you live alone? Or ..." she let it dangle.

"Kind of. My parents moved to Antigua four years ago. I've lived alone in their house ever since. But I spend a lot of time with my agent. She'll probably be staying with me — or with us — until it's time to go out on the road."

"I see." At least she wouldn't be alone with him. However convenient that was, remained to be seen.

"And you?" he asked. "Do you have a boyfriend where you came from, which was ..."

"Ottawa." She let out a little laugh. "And no, I don't have a boyfriend."

"I'm surprised. You're so beautiful."

She turned away quickly to hide her blush, though she couldn't remember smiling as widely in years. In truth, she'd never had a boyfriend to speak of. That this could be a mutual attraction seemed beyond the realm of possibility. She *had* to keep this one shining connection alive.

"There I go again, making you uncomfortable," he said, his concerned frown lightened by a small smile.

"Has anyone ever told you you're very charming?"

"They have, but I'm not trying to be. I'm only being truthful."

"Thank you, then. I think the last time anyone told me I looked beautiful was when I dressed up as a princess for Halloween at age eight."

"In that case, get used to it, because as my assistant

you'll be dressed like a princess every time we perform."

"Sounds like fun," she said. "Much more glamorous than shoveling horse poo."

He laughed. "And you'll still get to be around horses."

"It's surprising you're single too." A lump rose in her throat as she realized she'd made an assumption. The lump deflated a little when he confirmed her thought.

"Would you believe I've been waiting for the right girl to come along?" He made eye contact and rendered her incapable of speech at the implication. "I've been single for a couple of months. It wasn't really meant to last."

She forced her excitement down to a simmer so she could talk without squealing like a little girl. "Tell me more about the job. Where do you perform magic?"

"I've been out of the country for the past two years, performing in the U.S., and before that, Japan."

"Miami. Right."

"But I'm planning a Canada-wide tour. I'm from here originally. I grew up in Kingston."

"You have some pretty big audiences?"

"Some, yes."

She swallowed hard. "Can you teach me how to get over stage fright while you're teaching me what to do to assist you?"

"It won't be a problem, if you trust me."

Herman thought she'd follow him to the ends of the earth and trust him with her life, but what came out of her mouth was, "I think I can do that."

"Excellent." He smiled and she grinned back, feeling giddily like she'd somehow made it onto a train bound for a world that existed beyond the realm of all her wildest dreams.

CHAPTER 2

When the train stopped at Kingston station, Stephen stood and waited in the aisle for Herman to slide out of her seat. With her backpack over her shoulder, and clutching her blue paper flower tightly by its paper stalk, she looked up at him. He smiled at her warmly, dissolving her qualms for the moment. She waited on the platform while he retrieved a small black overnight bag. She expected to head directly to the parking lot, but instead he led the way into the station.

Keeping up with his lengthy stride between the rows of empty blue and red seats, she fought the compulsion to face the embarrassment of changing her mind. Even with the lump in her throat, it was easier to allow the momentum to carry her along, for better or for worse. There was something about Stephen, something about his commanding appearance and his confidence that made her believe she could trust him, even as she remembered there was a reason young girls shouldn't talk to strangers.

They exited the other side of the station through sliding glass doors and Stephen stopped just outside. Lined up were a number of taxis, a few cars, and one white limousine that advanced as Stephen watched. The car came to a halt in the middle of the roadway in front of them, and the driver came around to the passenger side.

Stephen stepped off the curb with one hand on Herman's back; his touch sent waves of electricity up and down her spine.

The man bowed slightly and said, "Good morning, Mr.

Dagmar." Stephen nodded and gave the uniformed man his bags. Herman followed suit. She took Stephen's outstretched hand in hers as she climbed into the cavernous burgundy leather enclosure ahead of him. Sliding across the seat, she noted the contrast of fragrant interior to the odor of exhaust outside.

"How famous are you?" she asked Stephen once he was settled in beside her. She felt slightly reassured knowing they weren't alone.

"I'm not famous at all in Canada. Yet." He grinned. "Most of my money comes from my family."

As the limo pulled away from the station and turned onto the street, Herman looked out the rear window and thought, *Here goes nothing.*

"Don't worry, Herman," Stephen gently intoned. "You're safe."

Herman scratched her head. "Do you live in a mansion?"

"No, just a house. It's on a large property though."

The car glided down a road with houses on both sides. Before long they turned right, and Herman caught glimpses of a body of water out the driver's side window. Lake Ontario, or so she thought it must be. The choppy, deep-gray expanse of lake stretched, in some places, as far as the eye could see. For a while it seemed as though they might stop within the comfort of one of the little clusters of homes they passed. Then the scenery became nothing but trees.

"You live out in the middle of nowhere?" Herman asked.

"We're almost there. Hopefully the weather will clear up so we can go for a horseback ride later, if you'd like."

"That would be nice."

The car slowed and turned into a long, paved driveway with sharply spiked, black iron gates open on both sides. A fence to match stretched beyond the shadows of trees that stood bare in the distance. At the end of the driveway stood an old Victorian-style two-story house.

The driver parked in the circular driveway in front of the house and came around to open the passenger-side door. Stephen got out first and extended his hand to help Herman out of the car. He allowed her the time to study her surroundings while the driver retrieved the bags. The dark red-brick house was tall and narrow. Curtains open in two of the front windows revealed a lamp situated in the middle of each. They reminded Herman of a story in which the lonely occupant kept a candle burning, waiting for a loved one to return from a long journey. Dead center, high above the front door like something out of a fairy tale, was a round turret. Around the mid-point of the cylinder, a row of stained-glass windows made it appear that the top could be lifted off by a giant hand. A thin post atop—probably a lightning rod—pointed to the gradually clearing sky. *Rapunzel* ran through her imagination, and she wondered with a shiver where the guest room was situated.

A ray of sunlight shone through the clouds from behind the house; a dark-suited man with salt-and-pepper hair and a gruff, pockmarked face materialized out of its shadow.

"Welcome home, Mr. Dagmar," the man said in a deep baritone voice as he bowed slightly to Stephen. "The ladies are waiting for you in the foyer."

"Thank you, Hawkins." Stephen turned to Herman and said, "This is Miss …"

"Anderson," Herman finished for him.

Stephen frowned at her briefly and then turned back to the man who she assumed was the butler. "This is Miss Anderson. I'd like to have the guest room made up for her in case she decides to stay."

"Yes, Sir," Hawkins said.

"Is Nina here today?"

"She is."

16

"Have her come to the dining room in five minutes, please."

"Of course, Sir." Hawkins hastened up the steps to the ornately carved front door and opened it.

Stephen picked up Herman's backpack. His bags had disappeared, taken into the house, presumably, by the chauffeur. He held out his other arm and smiled at her invitingly. "Shall we?"

Herman nodded and with the lump firmly stuck in her throat, she placed her hand on his bicep, noticing how hard it was under the fabric of his coat.

She expected to behold a grand foyer, and it *was* spectacular out of the corner of her eye, but what drew her attention were the ten or twelve beautiful women seated against the walls. They were all dressed as though they were waiting to enter a formal ball. The chatter amongst them ceased, and like a school of fish following in each other's wake, their eyes followed Stephen. Without a glance in either direction, he ushered Herman to the right of a long flight of stairs that split in two directions at a landing above, and into a room at the far end of the massive foyer through which they had entered. Stephen went through the door with Herman in the lead. He shut it behind him as she turned to face him.

"They would be the interviewees for the assistant's position," he explained.

"The same one you offered me?"

"Yes. I'm sorry I didn't mention it."

"They look ..." she searched for a word, thinking about her own comparatively grubby clothing. "... qualified."

"I don't care what their qualifications are. I want you."

She wilted on the spot.

"But no pressure," he continued. "I'll interview them anyway, just in case you decide not to stay."

"It would make me feel better if you have a backup

plan. Just in case," she said, feeling suddenly, inexplicably possessive of the job she wasn't sure she could handle.

"Okay," he said with a sigh. "In the meantime, there's a computer there all ready to go online if you'd like. Or if you want to see the rest of the house, Nina will be in to show you around. The kitchen is across the hall, and lunch will be on the table at twelve. And you can go up to the stables if you wish. I'll come to find you the moment I'm finished." He backed toward the door. "Are you okay?" he asked as he put down her backpack and turned the knob.

"I'm fine."

"Good. Someone will be in soon."

He stepped out the door and closed it behind him, only to open it again before Herman had a chance to turn away.

"I've got to ask," he said, popping his head back in. "Are you afraid of heights, water, or animals such as mice, rabbits, birds, and snakes?"

She thought about the list for a second and shook her head. "No," she replied.

"You were made for me," he said, blessing her with one of his radiant smiles before closing the door.

***

The moment Stephen stepped out the door, the foyer fell silent again. He didn't have to look at any of the interviewees perched, alert upon burgundy velvet-covered benches against both sides of the room, to know their eyes were on him. They were drawn to him as though he were a human magnet, just as Herman had been. He passed the stairs, turned right, and stepped into the dining room where his agent, Margaret, waited for him to arrive.

"Hey," she said without looking up. She sat poring over the applications that were strewn across the large antique dining room table. He closed the door behind him and leaned against it, staring at the top of her dark mane of hair shining in the light of the chandelier above her head. Her long, graceful fingers, poised to turn a page, were an elegant extension of the rest of her lithe body. Finally, she looked up and took in his appearance with icy-green eyes. She was every bit as beautiful as any of the women outside.

"What's the matter with you?" she asked. Being inseparable for five years, both as best friends and then co-workers, made it easy for her to tell when there was something different, however subtle, about him.

"I found her," Stephen said, his back still to the door.

"Who?"

"She has a perfect body and long, brown hair and the bluest eyes you've ever seen. And her lips! Full and beautiful. And the way they move when she speaks ... absolutely captivating."

Margaret narrowed her eyes. "You hired someone on the train again, didn't you?" It was a statement more than a question.

Stephen nodded.

"Okay," she said, sitting back in her chair. "Tell me more about her."

"I think she's running away from home. She has a job to go to, but she agreed to come and check this one out. She's sweet and innocent and she's almost eighteen."

Margaret crossed her arms and narrowed her eyes even more.

"No, I didn't audition her the same way I did the others," he said.

"So you didn't bang her in the limo on the way here."

"No! She's not of age. And anyway, I knew from the second I saw her that she's the one."

Margaret began to say something just as the door opened on the far side of the room to her left, and Nina came in from the kitchen. Both Stephen and Margaret glanced at the slight young woman and then at each other.

"Should I leave the two of you alone?" Margaret asked.

Stephen shook his head almost imperceptibly and walked over to have a quiet word with the girl. After a few seconds she bowed and backed out of the room, and Stephen turned back to his friend.

"Well then," Margaret said, throwing her hands up and glaring down at the stacks of paper in front of her. "Tell them all to go home."

"No, I still want to interview them."

"What the hell for?"

"Herman might not take the job."

Margaret raised her eyebrows. "*Herman*?"

"Yeah."

"Okay, let me get this straight. You're telling me she's the one you want but that she might not stay. I'm confused."

He stood, silently pleading with his friend to understand what he had only begun to comprehend himself.

"What the hell is *wrong* with you, Stephen? I've never seen you undone like this before …"

Margaret put her hand up to her mouth, realization dawning on her face. "Oh my God," she said quietly.

He closed his eyes as he spoke. "It doesn't matter whether or not she'll be my assistant, Margaret." He opened his eyes and swallowed hard. "She's the girl I'm going to marry."

.

Chapter 3

The sound of cooing birds beckoned Herman to the room's only window in search of the source. A protective line of tall, thick pines stood like sentries around the perimeter of a vast lawn, and the greens of daffodils and tulips poked their heads up through the soil below the window. Beyond the flower garden, a cobblestone walkway wide enough for two people to stroll side by side wound its way past a patio off to the left. To the right was a small, red-brick building with six or eight sides and many small windows near the top—a shed, or a coop, perhaps. She turned her back on the peaceful scenery outside to have a good look at the room. It appeared as domestically normal as the garden. Two of the dark paneled walls were adorned with painted landscapes, and the wall opposite the door had built-in bookshelves from hip-height to ceiling, containing fragrant old books. A computer with a large flat screen that sat upon a heavy, ancient-looking desk was the only evidence she hadn't stepped back in time.

Herman sat in the chair behind the desk. Staring out the window at the rolling clouds, she listened abstractly for noises coming from the foyer. There was nothing more than the occasional giggle.

Just the thought of being out in the foyer, waiting with the other women and hearing the titter of laughter when her name was called made her happy to be locked away in a room by herself. Herman was nine when the teasing over her name reached its peak. The girls her age were beginning to form crushes, and the boys wanted nothing to do with her. Who would want to be caught holding hands with "Herman the Man"? She pleaded with her parents to let her change her name to a girl's, but it was like they wanted her to stay single her whole life. It was a family tradition on her father's side, they said. Her father's sister, Herman's Aunt Harold, had a daughter named Rudolph.

She loved her parents, despite everything. She often remembered a time before her mom became ill when, every night, she'd sit in the wide sill of the bay window at the front of their house to wait for her dad to come home from work. The aromas from Mom's cooking wafted in from the kitchen, as the snow fluttered down past the street light. Red, green, blue, and yellow Christmas lights around the window glittered in multi-colored facets on the carpet of white beneath the window. Each evening when her father's car appeared up the street, she breathed a sigh of relief. She waved to him as he, tired from a day at the office, trudged up the steps to the front door. If it seemed he might not notice her sitting there, she'd knock on the window. He always smiled and waved, happy to see her. She would run to hug him before he even got his coat off. His jacket, wet and cold from the snow, smelled like the outdoors, muffling the scent of his Old Spice.

It was shortly after Herman's tenth birthday when her mother began to forget to feed her and her brother. At first her dad looked after everything. He became Mr. Mom, taking over all the household duties and driving Herman and Chad to school the way their mother used to. His days were occupied with doctor's visits, treatment plans, and simply trying to find out what was wrong. When he lost his job, he started drinking. Since then, Herman couldn't remember her dad without a drink in his hand.

She arrived home from school one snowy day just before Grade Five March Break to find her dad celebrating. A drug to stabilize her mother's condition had finally worked. Everything returned to normal for a while; her mom started looking after Herman and Chad and the house again. Her dad got a new job that he was excited about, except it took him away from home for weeks at a time.

By September, her mom started to fall back into the pattern of not caring about the housework. Herman tried to tell her dad, but it was as though he didn't care. He told her between slugs of alcohol that he needed his current job in order to keep them living in the manner to which they had become accustomed. This made no sense to an eleven-year-old Herman, but her dad said she was old enough to deal with it. So Herman learned to prepare meals for herself and five-year-old Chad. That was the way things remained until Herman's determination to make a better life for them, and force her father to notice that he needed to help, decided her. She started to teach Chad to look after himself.

It was after one of her father's long absences — six weeks, the longest to date — when Herman discovered something about him that she believed she would never tell another living soul. As it turned out, Stephen already knew.

CHAPTER 4

Nina was petite with ten-carat-gold-colored hair and the eyes of a startled fawn. She stepped into the room in ballet shoes like a young sprite, though she appeared to be about the same age as Herman. She was dressed in a form-fitting floral blouse and yellow pants that came to her calves, making Herman feel under-dressed in her clunky sweatshirt and slightly ripped jeans. Nina was so attractive that Herman couldn't imagine why Stephen wasn't with her. Or maybe he was. Whatever the case, Herman was immediately envious of the girl.

"I'm Nina," she said.

Herman stood as she muttered her name.

"I've been asked to show you your room. Or do you want something to eat or drink?" Nina held her hands behind her back when she spoke, like she was hiding something.

"Would I be eating alone? Or is Stephen …"

"Master Dagmar said that he wishes to dine with you tonight, but he won't be available for lunch. He sends his regrets," Nina said, smiling.

Master? Herman wondered what planet she'd landed on.

Something in the way the girl looked at her, as though she was a fly to be pinned to a board and de-winged, caused Herman to panic. "You know what, maybe it would be better if I just left," she said, picking up her backpack. When she looked up, Nina was frozen in place like a deer facing an oncoming set of headlights.

"Please, wait here one second." The girl held up a finger and backed out of the room, closing the door behind her.

The alarm in the servant's eyes triggered Herman's qualms again. If Stephen could provoke such fear in the people who worked in his house, then who the hell must he be? Herman didn't want to end up that way; she hadn't agreed to come with him to end up calling him "Mr." or even worse, "*Master* Dagmar." What she really hoped for was the feel of his lips touching hers. She didn't want to become part of his property.

She jumped when the door opened and Stephen himself walked into the room.

"Is there something wrong?" he asked.

"I just ..." Herman didn't know what to say. She shifted her eyes to Nina and Stephen's followed. Nina was staring at her feet, her face red.

He approached Herman slowly and reached out to take her hand. "I realize you must have a lot of questions, and I promise I'll answer all of them the second I'm done with the interviews." He looked her in the eye. "Will you stay, please?"

His sincerity made it impossible to refuse him. She nodded yes; suddenly she couldn't care less where it was all leading, as long as she could be near him.

"Thank you." He smiled and turned to leave.

"Wait!" said Herman, stopping him mid-stride.

He spun on his booted heel toward her, and she noticed how great he looked in his leather pants and black button-down shirt with lacy frills at the cuffs.

"I know I asked you this on the train, but now that I've seen all those beautiful women," she gestured toward the door, "I have to ask again. Why me?"

Stephen squinted, looking directly at her and beyond her at the same time. He snorted out a tiny laugh and shook his head slightly. "I'll explain later," he said with a genuine smile in his eyes. "Are you okay with that?"

"Sure."

"Good," he said, turning and walking out the door, leaving Nina in his wake, expectantly facing Herman.

"So, where to?" There was no friendliness left in Nina's voice.

"I guess I'll see my room," Herman said, feeling strangely as though she had won a battle.

***

Nina explained, amid the staring eyes of the throng of ladies in the foyer, that there were five rooms on the main floor. Next to the office where Herman had been installed was the living room. A glance through the door gave the impression that the room was decorated much like the office, but with a large-screen television instead of a computer. Above the mantle of a wide, well-used fireplace, hung a family portrait featuring parents, a black-haired little boy, and a baby in arms. On the opposite side of the elegant main staircase were the dining room and kitchen, and a small powder room.

Herman climbed the stairs two steps behind Nina, who was lugging her backpack like it weighed more than she did, feeling almost as awed by the house as she had been by its owner. A familiar stained-glass window, with a similar pattern to the row of windows around the turret, towered over the landing. The stairs continued up both to the left and right. Three steps more led to another landing on which there were doors, facing one another. Nina led the way up the left staircase and gestured over her shoulder, mumbling that her Master's office was on the opposite side. They turned left again to climb the rest of the way to the top floor. Herman's breath was stolen by a portrait on the wall facing her of an older, even more stunning version of Stephen.

"Is that—" she started to ask.

"That is Mr. Dagmar, Master's father," Nina interrupted. Having no experience with servants, Herman wondered if they were all as rude as Nina.

"The guest room is here," the girl said, leading the way down a hallway papered in a rich burgundy. A sparkling chandelier lit the way. At the opposite end, Herman spied a spiral staircase complete with an ornate lace iron railing. Halfway down the corridor, Nina stopped and pushed on the wall to her right. It wasn't until the wall began to move that Herman noticed the door. She turned to look at the wall opposite to see if there was a similar opening, but if there was, she couldn't find it.

Nina entered the room and stood with her back to the door, allowing Herman to precede her. A four-poster bed, with a cover of deep green, gold, and a touch of red, was surrounded by gauze curtains that hung from the black ceiling. This all contrasted with the smooth vanilla-cream-colored walls. The furniture was carved in a Gothic style. Lamps shaded with stained glass stood at each of the two windows like the ones she had seen downstairs from the outside. An area rug of forest green covered the floor almost all the way to the walls.

"If you want to freshen up ..." Nina stepped over to the wall to the right of the bed and pushed. Again, a door Herman wouldn't have seen opened to reveal a sparkling white bathroom with a large shower stall that sported not one, but two shower heads.

Even the bathroom made her want to pinch herself to make sure she was awake.

"Is everything okay?" Nina asked.

"Er, yeah, I guess." She shrugged, not wanting to seem too impressed in front of the girl. "I'll just be a minute."

"Would you like me to stay until you're ready to come down for lunch?"

"Would you mind?" asked Herman. She had no idea what to do first. Having few friends all her life had left her socially ill-equipped. Her experience with being in the house of someone she knew, let alone a complete stranger's, was limited.

"I'll be here when you come out," said Nina.

Herman splashed water on her face, wondering if she would get a tour of the rest of the rooms, particularly the one at the top of the spiral staircase. She thought again about the turret she had seen when they arrived in the car. *The limo.* She brushed out her hair with a large soft-bristled brush she found sitting beside the sink. Grimacing at herself in the mirror, she took a breath and prepared to face Nina again, determined to get whatever information she could.

"Who are the Dagmars?" Herman asked as she returned to the bedroom, thinking it best to start at the top. The stunned expression on Nina's face made Herman wonder if the girl would run off to find Stephen again; she thought it best to explain what she meant.

"Do they own a huge corporation or something?"

"The Dagmars have always had money."

"Why do you call him 'Master'? It seems a bit … medieval."

Nina held her nose in the air. "My family has worked for the Dagmars for generations. I inherited this job. I've always referred to him as 'Master.' Even when we were little. I treat him with respect. He deserves it."

"What makes him so special?"

"You'll find out. If you stay long enough."

"Why wouldn't I?" Herman asked, wondering what Nina was implying.

Nina narrowed her mouth as though berating herself internally.

"Of course you will stay," she said.

Herman decided to change the subject. Maybe the

28

house was a safer topic. "What's in the room at the back here?" she asked, pointing to the wall where the bathroom was situated.

"The room behind this wall is Master's wardrobe."

Herman raised her eyebrows.

"It's not only his own clothes he keeps in there. It's also the wardrobe for his shows. His assistant's clothes are in there, too."

"His assistant's clothes? You mean he has all of the dresses and things from his last assistant?"

"Yes, he buys them all himself. The cost of his wardrobe is extraordinary; there is no way an *assistant* could afford the clothes she wears in one of Master's shows."

Herman didn't like the way she said the word "assistant," as though it was a less desirable position than the one she herself held. "How does he know they'll fit?"

"Master Dagmar's assistants are all about the same size."

"Did you know Stephen asked me to be his new assistant?"

"Not until now, no." Nina's brief look of anger disappeared as quickly as it came, as she sized Herman up.

Herman felt incomparably large for a moment but it passed, though not without another bout of green envy. She was suddenly irritated at Stephen. Did he pick her up from the train just because she was the right size? Impossible. She tried to recall, without success, the proportions of the applicants downstairs. She hadn't a right to demand anything of him, or ask whether he had seen her only as the proper fit for a room full of clothing. He knew nothing about her, which brought her back to the same question: Why her? She wanted even more than before to talk to him.

"How many assistants has he had?" Herman wondered how desirable the job was, if it wasn't going to last long anyway.

"I'm really not sure. This is the first time Master has been home in over a year. But I believe he plans to stay here for a while now." Nina smiled her first genuine smile. "I think he has come home for good."

Herman gave her a black look and turned for the door. There was something creepy about the way the girl acted whenever she mentioned Stephen.

"What's at the top of the spiral staircase?" Herman asked, gazing up at it.

"That's Master's playroom. We don't go up there." Nina headed down the corridor and Herman followed, wondering if she was included in that particular "we."

CHAPTER 5

Stephen got up from the table the moment the door closed on the back of the last applicant, still sorting out papers as he prepared to leave.

"You're in a hurry," Margaret commented. "I was going to ask you if you'd like to have some lunch. It's almost one-thirty already."

"You go ahead. I'm going to look for Herman." He started toward the kitchen door but stopped when he heard a knock at the door through which the girls had been coming and going. It was Hawkins, come to announce a visitor. The Dagmar's administrator backed out as an elderly man with a marked hunch entered the room. His square, droopy face stretched into a smile when he saw Stephen.

"Gerald!" Stephen exclaimed, happy to see his grandfather's old friend.

He hastened across the room, remarkably spry for an octogenarian, and Stephen met him in the middle.

"Stephen, it's good to have you home," the old man said, hugging him and reaching up to gently slap his face.

"It's good to see you," Stephen said, smiling.

"And Marcy," Gerald said, with a knowing grin.

Margaret came around the table to kiss him on the cheek. "Gerald, you old tease. Just as charming as ever."

"As are you, my dear." He turned to Stephen. "Why haven't you made an honest woman of her yet?"

"He's not going to," Margaret said. "Besides, Stephen just found himself a new girlfriend this morning."

31

"Herman is hardly my girlfriend yet," Stephen said.

"Herman?" Gerald frowned. "You haven't switched sides, have you?"

Stephen laughed. "No, Herman is a girl. And so far, she has only agreed to be my assistant."

"Well," the old man lifted one bushy gray eyebrow. "We all know what that means."

"Not until she turns eighteen," Stephen said.

"When is that?"

"Three weeks from now."

Gerald chuckled. "You'll never last."

"He'll be keeping himself occupied, I'm sure." Margaret gazed at Stephen, understanding passing between them like a wireless current.

"Margaret and I were just talking about lunch," Stephen said, quickly changing the subject. "Would you like to join us, Gerald?"

"I was on my way to see a client. Even at my age, a lawyer's work is never done. I wouldn't say no to an invitation to dinner though."

"In that case, we'll see you at seven?"

"I shall return," Gerald said, holding out his hand for Stephen to shake it. "It's great to have you home."

"It's great to be back."

"See you later, Marcy," Gerald said with a cheeky smile and a wave on his way out the door.

Margaret laughed. "Bye, Gerald."

She turned to Stephen. He stood in the middle of the room, his mouth open and his palms turned upward.

"Go," she sighed.

"Thank you." He stepped toward her and bent to give her a quick peck on the cheek before he hurried out the kitchen door to find Herman.

CHAPTER 6

It was after twelve o'clock when Herman wandered from the office where Nina had left her, into the kitchen for lunch. A sturdy, rectangular chopping-block table that sat apart from where the action was taking place in the fully staffed cooking area awaited her, laden with sandwiches, fruit, and cakes of all kinds. She seated herself at the table facing the door to the dining room where she knew Stephen was conducting his interviews, hoping it would open and she would catch a glimpse of him, but no one went in nor out. As hard as she tried, she couldn't hear a thing coming from that direction. She ate slowly, thinking he might finish earlier than expected and come to join her.

It occurred to Herman that Nina was doing precisely what she herself was. For at least half an hour, the girl did nothing but lean against the kitchen counter, watching the cooks make preparations for dinner. Unable to think of any reason to loiter about waiting, she decided to ask Nina if it would be okay to go out and explore a bit. Nina said of course she should go and hurried to find Herman's jacket. She shrugged it onto her shoulders and stepped through the door in the kitchen that led directly outside.

After the cozy warmth, the damp, cold air enveloped her, and she slipped her hands into her pockets. The clouds had returned with a hint of drizzle. Straight ahead, past the perimeter of the groomed side yard, she spied the barn. She set off in that direction. The pungent odor of damp hay mixed with manure reached her and she breathed in deeply. Horse camp had been a childhood luxury she held close to her heart—a memory of the time before her mother's illness restricted her activities to nothing. She anticipated the fragrance of horsehide and leather with glee.

Herman stopped at the door of the barn and allowed her eyes to adjust to the darkness of the stables. Instead of the equine greeting she expected, she spied a man in a cowboy hat leaning against a beam, holding a pitchfork. He regarded her, unmoving, as if afraid to scare her away.

She was about to turn and leave when he spoke.

"Hello." He straightened and strode toward her, leaving the pitchfork behind. "I'm Reed," he said as he removed his hat and held out his hand.

Herman was confused. The young man she was shaking hands with resembled Stephen so much that they had to be related. But why, if he was rich like Stephen, was he in the barn holding a pitchfork as though he worked there? He looked at her with Stephen's kind, yet piercing, dark-colored eyes; his nose and mouth were less pronounced and his jaw was less square. His hair, unlike Stephen's, was brown. All of this gave her the impression that she was seeing a slightly younger, watered-down version of the man she met earlier on the train. Nevertheless, she imagined she would consider him the most gorgeous man alive if she hadn't already met Stephen.

"I'm Herman," she said, wondering how many more people she would have to introduce herself to. Reed didn't seem as much of a chore to get along with as Nina. His welcome smile was open and friendly.

"There are no horses in here," he said, returning his hat to his head. "I assume you were looking for horses."

"Yeah. Can you point me to where they are?"

"How about I show you? I'm almost finished up here."

"I don't want to take you away from your work."

"No problem. They need to come in anyway," he said. The way he turned on his booted heel made her think again of Stephen.

They walked together to the rear of the barn and through a door wide enough to accommodate a tractor. Six almost identical horses grazed on the new spring grass behind a fence a short distance away.

"Looks like a few have wandered off," said Reed.

"They're beautiful. How many are there?"

"Nine altogether." He nodded, his hand on his hip, gazing out at the animals.

"Can I help you bring them in?"

"Sure. Do you have any experience with horses?"

"A little."

"Great," he said, turning back to the barn. "I'll be back."

Herman strolled across the barnyard to the fence and held out her hand to the nearest horse. Ears alert, it pressed its nose to her palm and sniffed. Finding nothing there, it lowered its head to the grass. All six had sleek, dark brown bodies, and black manes and tails that swished back and forth occasionally in the stillness of the afternoon. The munching of the horses and the faint sound of water being sprayed from a hose were all that broke the silence. Soon the water stopped, and she turned to see Reed stride out of the barn toward her.

"Ready?" he asked, smiling.

"Yeah."

She followed him to the paddock gate, admiring the easy way he walked, relaxed and comfortable and in his element. He tied the gate open and they passed through. Even though Herman watched him put his pinkies in the corners of his mouth, she wasn't prepared for the extended, high-pitched whistle that came out. When he took a breath she heard, like a distant earthquake, the sound of galloping hooves. Through the mist, a dark blur thundered into view around a cluster of tall shrubs to her left. Three black beasts with long manes, all of them heavier than their stable-mates, approached at a gallop, showing no sign of slowing down. Herman pressed her back against the fence and silently begged not to be trampled. She looked to Reed for help but he simply nodded to her. The three strays ran through the gate one at a time and came to a skidding halt before the barn door. They trotted in, disappearing in a hairy whirl. Four of the six others followed them on their own. Reed went to retrieve the remaining two.

He offered to let her lead one of them, and Herman unplastered herself from the fence.

"Thank you," she said, taking the rope.

"Gorgeous animals, aren't they?"

"All of them are. Are any of them stallions?"

Reed smiled and shook his head. "No. All these horses are mares. We keep the stallions separate. When they're here that is. They're out at the moment."

Herman frowned a bit. "What, did they go out for coffee or something?"

Reed chuckled. "No, we lend them out for breeding purposes. For a fee, of course."

"Ah, prostitute horses," said Herman.

"I guess they are. I never thought about it that way before. Thank you for opening my eyes to a wider world." He bowed, making her giggle.

"Why do the Dagmars keep so many horses?" she asked, stroking the nose of the one she was holding.

"The six bays—the brown ones—are strictly for breeding. The three blacks—the Friesians—Mr. Dagmar uses to ride and use in his shows."

"Oh, not you too," she said, snapping her mouth shut the second the words came out. Reed looked at her but said nothing.

"It's just, it seems ... I mean, everyone I've met today calls him 'Mr. Dagmar,' or 'Master,' of all things. He introduced himself as Stephen, but it seems like I'm the only one with the privilege of calling him that." Herman sighed. "I guess I'm a bit confused."

They arrived at the barn door, and Reed entered first with his horse. He guided the animal into the nearest stall to his right and took hers, propelling it toward a door on the left. It walked in, turned its massive body, and plunged its nose into a bucket hanging near the stall door. Reed closed both doors without saying a word. Herman started to wonder if she had crossed a line so bad that she'd be kicked out.

Finally, he turned to her. "You're confused about the way of things?" He raised his eyebrows but didn't give her a chance to reply. "Allow me to help you, milady."

Herman smiled and breathed a little more easily.

"The Currys—my family—have been with the Dagmars for generations. My mother is their housekeeper. You wouldn't have met her; it's her day off. Hawkins is my dad. He takes care of all the administration duties. And the one who calls him 'Master' is Nina, my sister. It's old-fashioned, I know. My friends think I'm weird to want to stay here to work, but hey," he waved his hand around as if to present the barn to her, "who wouldn't? You, on the other hand, are Mr. Dagmar's guest, I assume?"

"About to become his employee. He invited me to be his assistant. Does that mean I'll have to call him 'Mr. Dagmar,' too?"

"No," replied Reed. "He works very closely with his assistants."

Herman flushed and stared at her shoes, wondering for the umpteenth time if she had taken on more than she could handle.

"Don't worry about it," he said, seeming to understand where she was coming from. "Anything you need, don't ever hesitate to ask any of us. And Mr. Dagmar is easy-going. In fact, he's really nice once you get to know him."

She felt herself relax for the first time since she arrived. "Thank you," she said.

"Let's go settle the rest of the horses in their stalls, then?"

"Sure."

Herman walked down the right side of the barn, closing the stall doors as she went, and Reed took the left.

When they reached the far end of the barn where Herman had first come in, Stephen stepped out of the shadows.

"I see you've met Reed," he said. He grinned as he sauntered toward her. The butterflies in her stomach fluttered at seeing him again.

"Yeah." She glanced at the young man, frozen by her side in the deer-in-the-headlights pose that appeared to be reserved for the servants. She didn't think she was quite that bad.

"I hope he's been helpful," Stephen said. Then to Reed he asked, "You're doing well?"

Reed had the look of a puppy, excited to see its master but afraid of the consequences of jumping up to greet him.

"Yes, thank you. I'm happy to see you home again, Sir." He smiled tentatively as if trying the expression on for size and then seemed to think better of it, which left him with a lopsided grin. The sight gave Herman the impression she was looking at one man in a mirror instead of two different males of different families. Vastly different, if Reed was to be believed.

"Thank you, it's good to be back," said Stephen. He turned to Herman as though dismissing the other man entirely from his mind.

"Have you had enough of the horses yet, or would you like to stay longer?" he asked her politely.

"Did you have anything else you wanted to do?"

"I do, in fact. I was going to suggest a ride, but it's starting to rain again. So, if you'd like to take the carriage, and you don't mind the dampness outside for a little while, I'll show you where I work when I'm at home."

"Sure," she said, nodding. "That would be nice."

"I should tell you first, where we are going is rather remote. Would you feel more comfortable taking someone with us? Reed could come, or Nina, if you don't want to go alone."

"No, it's fine," Herman said, appreciating the offer. "I don't mind."

Stephen graced her with a heart-warming smile.

"Reed, would you mind getting the covered carriage ready? We'll take whichever of the Friesians is finished her lunch first."

"Of course," he said and hurried off.

Herman followed Stephen to a stall where one of the big black mares was munching her oats. She noticed vaguely that Reed was moving around the barn behind them while Stephen engaged her in conversation.

"My parents sent me to horse camp when I was younger," she told him. "It was the highlight of my childhood."

"I'm glad you're comfortable around them. I'm not sure if I'll take them on this tour. I'm working on some new material."

As Stephen told her about his show, his warmth melted any remaining nervousness she felt at landing in such an incredible situation. The incredibly gorgeous man at her side was slowly making her as comfortable around him as she was with the horses.

CHAPTER 7

The pattering rain had slowed again to a drizzle. But for the swish and rustle of the horse's movements in the harness, the tree-lined path they rolled along was still. Herman imagined birds huddled in the branches along the narrow roadway, puffed up against the dampness of the air, unwilling to move or sing. Early grass had begun to grow in the rut between the wheel tracks and delicate points along each twig promised buds of leaves. A faint mist clung to the ground, giving the appearance that it was raining from the ground, up. After several minutes of companionable silence, they reached a spot where the trees thinned and then opened up to a clearing.

"We're almost there," Stephen said.

As they rounded a bend, Herman was surprised to see a transport trailer parked beside a building that, itself, looked oddly out of place.

"It used to be a train station," he told her, and she nodded. That was it. There were no train tracks to be seen.

On the far side of the building, a long, gently sloping hill ended in a grassy bank at the waterline.

"Does your property come all the way out here?"

"All the way to the lake. We also own a small island out there," he waved his hand in that direction. When she squinted, she was able to see the faint outline of a landmass with trees through the misty air that hovered like an insubstantial wall over the water. Terrible with distances, she thought it couldn't be too far away, but it wasn't close enough to swim to, either.

Stephen stopped the horse and hopped down to tie her to a post. He came back and held his hand out to take Herman's as she stepped off the carriage. She followed him up a wide flight of painted wooden steps to the door of the old train station. He opened both of the tall double doors and reached around to turn on a light switch. The lights, suspended from the high ceiling, revealed a well-preserved waiting room. The ticket wicket was there, so were the long benches, their wood worn down by decades if not more than a century's worth of the pants and skirts of many generations. Sturdy wooden beams supported the ceiling; the walls were painted dark green.

"It's beautiful," Herman said. "I've always loved train stations."

"Me too. I found this one up for sale and I couldn't resist, so I bought it and had it moved out here." He looked around the room, as though seeing it for the first time. "I love the romanticism of a train station."

"Yeah," said Herman, awed at the thought of just being able to buy a train station. "Think of all the people who have said goodbye. All the re-united lovers."

She noticed Stephen gazing at her, smiling.

She grinned back. "What?"

"I'm glad to find we have something in common. Come with me." He tilted his head toward the ticket booth.

They entered the back room through a door marked "Employees Only" to the right of the wicket. Large crates were stacked around the walls of this, a larger, higher-ceilinged room than the one they had just left. Gold, silver, red, green, and blue chambers and props spilled out of the crates and sparkled in the light of the bare incandescent lights that hung unshaded from the beams above. Herman took it in silently.

"I'll teach you what all of this is for. If you decide to take the job."

41

She didn't answer right away.

"You're afraid. What of?" Stephen asked her gently.

"All of it, I guess."

"Why don't we sit down and talk about it?" He guided her to two armchairs placed up against the rear wall of the ticket office. A small, round wooden table sat between the chairs, at arm's reach of them both.

Herman eased herself into a chair and waited for him to speak.

"At the risk of scaring you off completely …" He trailed off his sentence while he searched either her face or his mind for the words he wanted to say next.

He started again. "Do you believe there is someone in the world for everybody?"

"I do."

"Because the moment I saw you, I knew that somehow this was meant to be."

"I know," she said. "I felt it too. But you've brought me to this incredibly different world I'm not used to. It's hard to believe it's true, you know?"

"I promise I won't rush you into anything. If you take the job, we'll focus only on that. Whatever makes you comfortable. I don't want you to feel like you owe me anything. If anything, I owe you. For trusting me enough to get off the train with me, and for being open to trying something new."

"What I don't understand, though, is why you think I can even do the job. I have no experience at anything, let alone standing onstage in front of people, assisting you in a magic show."

"It's a feeling."

She waited for him to go on.

"Okay, I'm going to be honest with you." He shifted his feet and leaned his elbows on his knees. His posture alone made her tingle with desire from head to toe.

He looked her in the eye when he spoke. "Neither of my last two assistants—the one who was with me for a year in Japan, nor the one I had for the year I was in the U.S.—were among the applicants I interviewed. In fact, I met them both on trains. Weird, I know. I travel by train a lot. But the point is, I knew when I met them that they had what it took. It was like a connection. An energy between us. And I felt it again today, with you. I wasn't wrong about them, and I don't believe I'm wrong about you. I know you can assist me. I simply know it."

"I'm glad you have all this faith in me, because I'm totally lacking it. I think I know what you mean about the energy, though. It's almost like electricity."

He smiled. "It is, isn't it?"

"Actually, there's something I have to be honest with you about." *This is it,* she thought. *This is where he puts me back on the train.* She took a deep breath. "It's my little brother. I might need to go back to Ottawa to get him after I get settled."

"What about your parents?"

Herman shook her head. "My mom's sick, and my dad's … away. I'm hoping he might come home to stay, but I'm not holding my breath."

"How old is your brother?"

"Chad's eleven. He's an amateur magician himself."

Stephen smiled. "I'm sure we can work something out."

"Thank you." She relaxed a little, yet she still wasn't convinced that it was all really happening.

"You're still nervous."

It was as though he'd read her mind.

"I'm *afraid* to believe all this is real," she confessed. "I'm afraid I'm going to go to sleep and wake up and discover I got knocked out and it was all a dream. I'm afraid of getting hurt."

"Herman." He reached out his hand and took hers. She

found it warm and comforting, better than anything she had felt since her father was there to protect her as a child. "This is real. I am real. And I will do everything in my power to see you never get hurt."

"So, I should just give myself over to you? Because that's what this is starting to feel like." *Please say yes, please say yes …*

He smiled and gently rubbed the back of her hand with his thumb. "Let's take it slowly, okay? One thing at a time. I'm not going to pressure you into doing anything until you're ready. For now, would you like to learn a few magic tricks?"

"Sure," she said. "And thank you. I feel a bit better."

"I'm glad," Stephen said as he stood and pulled her gently from her chair.

They spent the next few hours consumed with magic. Much to Herman's surprise, she was a natural.

***

The ride back to the house was more animated than the ride out to "the station," as Stephen called it. Not only had the mist lifted, so had their spirits. Herman had agreed to take the job.

When they arrived at the barn, Reed was there to take the horse and carriage with a simple nod. The day was giving way to dark, and Stephen held out his arm to Herman for the stroll home. Her mouth began to water as they approached the house and a tart, tomato-y aroma of Italian cuisine wafted into the still evening air.

"I'll walk you to your room so you can change for dinner," Stephen said as they passed through the patio door at the back of the house.

"That would be nice, but I've got nothing to change into. I'm wearing basically all I brought with me." Herman looked down at her mostly denim outfit feeling self-conscious, not for the first time. She had no idea she would end up in a grand house at a dinner party when she left home.

"I'm sure we can find something else for you. I'll have Nina help you pick something out."

With that he was gone to the kitchen, leaving Herman standing inside the patio door. Seconds later he came out with Nina, and they climbed the stairs together.

At the first landing on the left, Stephen opened the door to a room filled with racks of clothing. A full-length mirror hung on one wall, and a single backless bench stood in the middle of the room.

"Choose anything," he said to Herman with a smile. "It's all yours." And then to Nina he said, "Take good care of her."

"I'll see you at dinner, Herman." He left with a wiggle of his fingers.

The door clicked shut and Herman looked to Nina.

"What am I supposed to wear for dinner?" she sighed, begrudging the need to ask the girl for help.

"Nothing too sparkly." Nina flicked through the selection as though she knew exactly what was there. "How about this?" She handed Herman a black dress with a V-neck and a cinched waistband.

"I'll need shoes to go with it, I guess?" asked Herman, accepting the dress.

"What size do you take?"

Nina found her a pair of heels. With attire in hand, Herman went to her room, to shower and change for a dinner that would alter the way she saw the life she thought she knew.

CHAPTER 8

Herman descended the grand staircase on her way to the dining room, amazed at how feminine she felt. The assortment of cosmetics in her room's bathroom included various shades of lipstick and eye makeup, as well as perfumed soaps and shampoos for her shower. It had taken her a few experimental tries before she was satisfied with her face, but by the time she was ready, she barely recognized herself in the full-length mirror at the end of her bed.

She turned right at the foot of the staircase and found the dining room glowing warmly in the light of an overhead chandelier and dozens of candles. Stephen sat at the head of the table talking with an elderly gentleman to his left and a dark-haired woman, about the same age as Stephen, who sat across the table on his right, one chair away from him. The woman noticed Herman standing in the doorway and touched his sleeve.

He looked up and bedazzled her with his brilliant smile. "There's Herman," he announced. He met her halfway to the table, exquisite in a black suit and underneath, a white shirt with fine lace ruffles down the front. His black hair shone, even in the dimness of the room.

He took her hand and whispered in her ear, "You look beautiful," making her shiver.

"So do you," she whispered back, though she wasn't sure he heard her. He led her around the table to make introductions to his other guests.

"Herman, this is Gerald, a dear friend of the family,"

THE MAGICIAN'S CURSE

said Stephen, nodding toward the gentleman who rose from the table. He reached out a hand to shake Herman's.

"And this is Margaret, my agent and also my best friend. Margaret, this is Herman."

"Very nice to meet you," said Margaret as she smiled.

"Nice to meet you, too." Herman hoped the quiver in her voice wasn't obvious.

"Please, have a seat." Stephen pulled out the chair directly to the right of his.

Herman sat, keeping her hands on her lap, afraid to touch anything on the immaculately laid table. A burgundy tablecloth with white napkins and silver-trimmed white plates, gleaming silver cutlery, and sparkling crystal wine glasses were spread out before her the way she imagined they might be for a queen. She suddenly felt small and insignificant.

Stephen seated himself again. She was surprised that he spoke to her first.

"Do you like red wine?"

"Sure," said Herman, hoping she would.

Stephen poured her a glass and picked up his own.

"We have some celebrating to do tonight!" he declared. They all lifted their glasses and Herman did, too.

"Here's to new friends," he smiled at Herman, "and to old," he looked to Gerald and to Margaret. "And to coming home." He clinked glasses with Herman and then with the others.

"Hear, hear," said Gerald and Margaret in unison.

Herman sipped with the rest of them and felt the rich aroma of the wine rise up through her sinuses as it glided down her throat. The taste was wonderful, like everything else she had experienced on this eventful day. She thought she might be able to relax, eventually. As long as Stephen was beside her, she felt she had nothing to fear.

"How are you enjoying yourself here, so far?" asked

Gerald of Herman.

"It's very nice," she said, a little shocked at being the object of conversation.

"And very overwhelming," added Margaret helpfully.

Herman looked at her and smiled tentatively, unsure whether or not to agree.

"Don't worry, Herman, you'll get used to it," the older woman reassured her. "I remember the first time Stephen brought me here. It was like stepping into a fairy tale. And you haven't even seen him do any magic yet." Her eyes flicked in Stephen's direction. "Has she?"

"A little. Just some of the easy stuff," said Stephen.

"He's a brilliant magician," said Gerald. "One of the best there is."

"Gerald is my biggest fan," said Stephen. "But I suspect that may be because I feed him his favorite meal whenever I come home."

"He makes it himself, I'm told, though I don't think I've ever seen him in the kitchen," Gerald said with a chuckle.

"I just stand in the doorway and wave my wand and *voila*! Dinner is ready."

Margaret leaned close to stage-whisper to Herman. "Stephen is a huge show-off, but you'll get used to that too."

"I think I already am," Herman stage-whispered back.

Stephen and Gerald laughed.

"I think she's going to fit right in," said Gerald to Stephen.

"So do I," the younger man agreed. He lifted his glass to Herman.

As they drank, the door to the kitchen opened and a plump woman in an apron over an old-fashioned-style dress came through carrying a large bowl of salad, followed by Nina with a cheese grinder. Using silver tongs, the woman served Margaret first. Nina offered the cheese and

Margaret nodded.

Next the woman came to Herman and arranged the salad on her plate. Nina raised her eyebrows when it was her turn. Herman hesitated for a second, not sure if she wanted any.

"Would you like some cheese, Herman?" asked Nina.

"Nina!" Stephen hissed, glaring at the young woman.

Herman blushed and looked down at her lap, wishing the floor would swallow her. Beside her she heard Margaret whisper, "Oh shit," under her breath. The woman serving the salad finished with Stephen's and Gerald's plates, placed the bowl on the table, and hurried out of the room.

"You will address Miss Anderson properly," Stephen said to Nina when the door to the kitchen closed.

"Did you say 'Anderson'?" Margaret asked. She glanced at Herman and then at Stephen. He took the cheese grinder from Nina's hands and waved her off.

"Of course," said Stephen. "That's where I recognized her from."

"What?" Herman demanded. looking back and forth between Stephen and Margaret. Both stared at her oddly.

"Your father's name is George Anderson, isn't it?" Stephen said more than asked.

"How do you know my father?"

Out of the corner of her eye she saw Margaret nod at Stephen.

"I met him on the magician's circuit."

"But my father is a salesman." Herman frowned. "Does he supply you with something?"

Again, Stephen exchanged glances with Margaret.

"Do you know the name Paul Whitmore?" he asked.

"He's my dad's boss."

"Herman, your father isn't a salesman."

Herman frowned deeply. "What is he then?"

His eyes shifted back to Margaret almost imperceptibly.

"He's a magician." He cleared his throat. "Of sorts."

Herman fixed her eyes on the silver edge of her plate and the flickering shadow it made on the tablecloth from the light of a candle.

"This is a huge coincidence," she said softly to herself. She looked into the eyes of the man she'd met on the train. "This is a coincidence, isn't it?"

"Yes. Now I know why thought I recognized you. You resemble your father."

"I've been told that before," she said.

"But I only just put two and two together. I had no idea who you were when I sat down beside you this morning."

"I believe you," she said, looking him in the eye again. "Does this mean we might run into my dad?"

"I doubt we'll come across them until the magicians' convention in Ottawa next year."

"Them?"

"Your father and Paul," Stephen said.

Herman wondered if she should ask any more questions, but it seemed impolite to commandeer the dinner conversation.

"Are you okay?" Margaret asked her, for which she felt grateful.

"Yeah." She turned to Stephen. "Can we talk about this tomorrow?"

"Of course." His smile reassured her as it enveloped her in a sensation of safety.

"Oh good," said Gerald. "I'm starving."

***

The lasagna was every bit as delicious as Gerald had said it would be, and dessert was a dreamy lemon mousse. That Nina was nowhere to be seen for the rest of the evening made it perfect. Herman's self-consciousness dissolved with the easy conversation, the pleasant company, and the warm inclusion into Stephen's small circle of friends. She hadn't felt so at home since her own family was intact and free of her mother's disease.

It was past eleven o'clock when they stood at the front door to bid Gerald a good night. She glanced at the stairs, hoping Stephen would carry her up to bed and wish her pleasant dreams with a tender kiss on the lips like Prince Charming, but she suspected he was far too much a gentleman. After they waved goodbye to Gerald, Stephen turned to Margaret.

"Did you decide on a hotel for tonight or are you staying here? The playroom is ready for you, or you can stay in my room."

Herman frowned before she could stop herself. Stephen's quick eye picked up on it.

"I have a huge bedroom. Half of it is an office with a fold-out sofa," he explained. "The two sections are separated for privacy. Margaret has crashed there on more than one occasion, when we've been working late."

"I see," Herman said. "Not that it matters ..."

"It matters to me what you think."

"Actually," Margaret said, giving Stephen a strange look, like he should have known better than to ask, "I already took the liberty of having Hawkins take my bags up to the playroom. The futon up there is much more comfortable."

"Great," said Stephen.

"I'm happy you're staying, too," said Herman to Margaret. "I'd love to talk to you more tomorrow if I can."

"About what?" asked Margaret.

"Oh, you know. Stuff."

"I'll tell you anything you want to know." Margaret smiled at her knowingly.

"Well," Margaret went on, "I'll be off then. Don't you two stay up too late."

The older woman climbed the stairs with a wave, and Herman looked to Stephen.

"Is there anything you'd like to take up to bed with you?" he offered. "A cup of tea, maybe?"

"That's a good idea."

He took her hand and led her to the kitchen. She sat at the table while he spoke to the staff, who were still cleaning up from dinner, about breakfast. He carried her tea in a china mug as they trod up the stairs slowly, side by side, in silence. When they stopped at Herman's door, she leaned against it and faced him.

"Thank you," Stephen said with a contented smile. He held the mug with both hands as though he was trying not to touch her.

"Thank you? You're thanking me? Shouldn't it be the other way around?"

"We could thank each other I suppose." He stood close and gazed at her in the dim light of the hallway. The red glow in his eyes made her think of fire, comforting and dangerous at the same time. "But I do want to thank you for being here," he continued, "and for agreeing to be my assistant. I also want to thank you for your company. It's been the most pleasant evening I've had in a while."

"Me too," said Herman. "Tonight was the first time I've felt like I belonged somewhere in a long, long time."

He leaned forward and kissed her then, lightly on the forehead.

"Sweet dreams, Herman." He left her holding the mug she hadn't even realized he'd handed her. She felt along the wall until she found the knob for her bedroom door.

As she lay under heavy covers, the last thing she thought of was the gentle touch of Stephen's lips.

***

Stephen entered his room through the door in the

staircase, which opened on the office part of his vast bedroom. A single candle on the table beside the fold-out bed revealed a feminine shape beneath the covers.

"Right," he whispered under his breath.

He stared into the eyes of the woman in his spare bed.

"Let's get this over and done with," he said as he took off his jacket. He blew out the candle and climbed onto the bed beside her.

CHAPTER 9

Stephen woke up alone at six-thirty the next morning in his own bed. After a quick shower, he threw on an old pair of black jeans and a t-shirt and hurried down the stairs in hopes of speaking to Margaret before Herman got up. Margaret was in the kitchen, poring over a stack of papers and munching on a piece of buttered brown toast.

"How was the playroom?" he asked her.

She tilted her head toward him before her eyes lifted from the page she was reading. "Playful." She smiled. "How did you sleep?"

"Not well. Listen, can we go into the dining room? We need to talk." He looked around at the kitchen staff, politely ignoring him as they worked.

"Sure." She picked up her plate in one hand and the stack of papers in the other, and proceeded to the dining room table while he made sure the door was properly shut between the rooms.

"What's up?" she asked as he sat at the head of the table.

"I need a favor."

"Anything. Name it."

"I need you to help me find ways to keep Herman busy while I take care of family business."

"Is that what we're calling it these days?" she asked. "The 'family business'?"

"I'm hoping it won't take long, now that Herman is in the picture." He stared at the tablecloth and bit his fingernail.

Margaret touched his other hand. "She really is special, isn't she?"

"Yeah."

"You know you're going to have to tell her about the 'family business' sooner or later."

"I'd rather wait until I have to." He raised his gaze to Margaret's face. "Do you think that's a good idea?"

"If you don't want to scare her off before she even gets a chance to get to know you, then yes. Wait a bit."

Stephen looked back down.

"Stop berating yourself." She leaned toward him. "It's not like there's any choice in the matter."

A small knock came from the door to the kitchen.

"Lotta!" said Margaret as the door opened. Stephen spun around and stood to greet the head housekeeper and matriarch of the Curry family.

"Mr. Dagmar, it's so nice to have you home," said the small, stout woman with silver-streaked red hair. She stepped into Stephen's outstretched arms for a brief embrace.

"It's great to see you again. But I wasn't expecting you until tomorrow. Isn't today your day off?"

"It is, Mr. Dagmar, but Nina was very tired this morning, so I agreed to come in so she could sleep a little longer. I hope you don't mind. And besides," she said without pause, "it was all I could do to stay away yesterday, knowing you were back. Now what can I get for your breakfast?"

She peeked around him at the level of his lower ribs to see the table.

"Oh! You don't even have a pot of coffee! I'll get that right away." She disappeared through the door to the kitchen in a flurry of hands and apron.

"Well, she hasn't changed a bit," said Margaret.

"Some things don't." He sat again at the table.

"Would you like me to take Herman shopping today?"

"That's a good idea. She can't have brought much in her backpack, and she can't live in show clothes."

"So, jeans and then the lingerie department?" She smiled at Stephen wickedly. "I know what you like."

"I thought we agreed on *not* scaring her off." He smiled back.

"Fine then. I guess the lingerie can wait for your wedding night."

From the direction of the kitchen came a sudden *yip!* of surprise, and Lotta almost dropped a tray of coffee and pastries at the entrance to the dining room. She made it to the table safely, however. She chattered about the weather and other minutiae as she set the table and poured coffee for Stephen and Margaret, as though she had heard nothing upon entering the room. Stephen asked her to close the door behind her when she left.

"Will I ever have a life of my own?" he moaned.

"That's why we spend so much time on the road. It'll be over soon, and yes, you'll have the life you want. You'll see."

"Hmm. So, about Herman," he said, returning to what was foremost on his mind. "She seemed to be getting along well with Reed yesterday."

"Perfect," said Margaret. "I'll take her out to the stable after shopping and lunch, and see that Reed keeps her occupied until dinner. That will leave me free to do whatever else you need of me."

"Margaret, I don't know what I'd do without you." He placed his hand on hers.

"Stephen, as long as you let me stay in your playroom, I'm all yours," she said, smiling.

"Done."

"So now, eat your breakfast, young Master, and then get done whatever you need to do."

He frowned.

"Don't worry, everything here will be taken care of," she said.

"Never mind the playroom, you can have the house."

She laughed, picked up a croissant and stuck it in his mouth.

"Eat," she said, and he ripped off a piece with his teeth. "Oh, just one thing."

Stephen raised his eyebrows as he chewed.

"What do I say to Herman if she asks about her dear ol' dad?"

Stephen finished his mouthful of croissant before answering her. "I guess, tell her about him."

"Not everything, surely."

Stephen considered the question again. "You're right. Maybe it should come directly from him, if she is to find out what he's capable of."

"Unless it runs in the family, in which case you might bring it out in her yourself."

"True," Stephen said, thinking. "Power like that does tend to be handed down through generations."

"You're proof of that."

"Okay then," said Stephen. "Tell Herman only the bare minimum about George if she asks. I'll tell her the rest."

CHAPTER 10

Three hours and nine stores from the time Herman had finally dragged herself out of bed that morning, she and Margaret sat down for lunch in a restaurant classier than any Herman thought she might have ever walked past. She hadn't owned so many clothes in her life; Margaret kept insisting that she take whatever she liked, and Herman didn't want to refuse, in case it seemed impolite. Or so she rationalized to herself.

Throughout the morning, Herman had been consumed by thoughts of Stephen. She recalled his smile, his natural masculine scent when he stood close to her, and the sound of his voice, deeper when he spoke quietly to her. Having been put in the care of his agent and best friend was almost as good as being with him. She had relentlessly pummeled Margaret with questions about him, feeling more at ease with the woman as the morning progressed.

They ordered coffees and salads and discussed what they had and hadn't bought.

"I still think you should have picked up the baby doll set with the garter belt," Margaret said with a wink.

"But who would I wear it for?" Herman batted her eyelashes in mock-innocence.

Margaret smiled over the lip of her coffee cup. "Oh, you never know."

"Do you really think Stephen likes me *that* way?"

Margaret nodded slowly, still smiling. "But don't be discouraged if he doesn't come out and show it right away.

Stephen is the sort of person who thinks things through *most* of the time. I know it seems impulsive of him to bring you home just like that," Margaret snapped her fingers. "I guess you could say he doesn't do things unless he's relatively sure of the outcome."

"Then why would he hesitate to start a relationship with someone he likes?"

Margaret took her time answering. "All I can say is that Stephen's life is extremely complicated right now. And knowing him the way I do, I know he'll want to make sure there's every chance of success in a romance with you as he can."

Herman couldn't help grinning.

"But be patient with him," Margaret went on. "Stephen sees something in you."

"Apart from my resemblance to my dad?"

"Definitely."

"Did you meet him? My dad?"

"Yes," Margaret said simply.

"But you don't want to talk about it."

Herman sat back in her chair as the waiter set their salads on the table. She had to wait for Margaret's response.

"It's not that I don't want to," Margaret finally answered. "It's just ..."

"Stephen would be more qualified to talk about him, them both being magicians and all," Herman interrupted.

"Right."

That topic dead, Herman moved on to the next. "How did you and Stephen meet?"

"We met in a bar I was working at when we were both going to Queen's University. He recognized me. He'd seen me around campus."

Herman frowned. "How long ago was that?"

"About five years ago."

"Five years?" Herman did the math. "How old is he

really?"

"He's twenty-three. Isn't that what he told you?"

"He started university early then?"

"When he was seventeen. He graduated at the top of his class in psychology at twenty."

"Wow," whispered Herman.

"He grew up fast for many reasons, least of which was the fact that his parents left him as master of the household while he was still a teenager."

"It's scary they left him with Nina." Herman clamped her hand over her mouth; the words had escaped before she had a chance to rein them in. Margaret looked up sharply from her lunch, and she wondered if she'd overstepped her bounds.

"You have a problem with Nina?" A glint in the older woman's eye told her it was okay to speak her mind.

"I don't know. Maybe it's just me, but it seems like half the time she acts as though she owns the place, yet when Stephen's around she's like a lapdog."

Margaret, about to swallow a mouthful of coffee, laughed and choked at the same time. She picked up a napkin and held it over her mouth.

"That's very astute of you," she said, wiping the tears from her eyes once she managed to stop coughing and compose herself. "I like you, you know." Margaret smiled. "You're intuitive."

"Thank you. I like you, too." She leaned across the table. "Speaking of intuition, there's something I'm having a feeling about right now."

Margaret leaned forward to whisper, "What's that?"

"There are three women on the other side of the room looking at you and giggling. I think they know you."

Margaret glanced in the direction that Herman had indicated with a flick of her eyebrows. "Oh God," she said, rolling her eyes.

"Who are they?" asked Herman.

"Stephen's fan club."

The trio stood, and like a cast of identical cartoon characters, shimmied their way over to Herman and Margaret.

"Margaret!" The skinniest—a pale blonde—dangled a limp hand, presumably to be shaken.

"Hello, Sadie," said Margaret, smiling politely.

"How's Stephen these days? He's in town, I guess?" She tittered. "He never goes anywhere without you!"

"Have you darlings formed another coven?" asked the freckled redhead to Sadie's left.

"No, we figured since we're attached at the hip, we'd start a Siamese Twin Society. Our motto is, 'Come Join Us.'"

The three cartoonish women laughed hysterically.

"Well, tell Stephen if he wants to get together, to give me a call," said Sadie, handing Margaret a post-it note with a phone number written on it.

Margaret took the yellow square of paper with a smile, and they watched the trio zigzag out the door, still giggling. She crumpled up the paper the moment they were out of sight. "Not bloody likely. I wouldn't waste his time."

"Not his type?" asked Herman, relieved that it could be true.

"Never has been, never will be," said Margaret.

"I wonder if I'm not either."

"What would make you think you're not?"

"Stephen is so highly educated, and here's me, a high school drop-out."

"But Herman, you have a head on your shoulders. That much is obvious." She touched Herman's sleeve. "You don't need a formal education for that.

"And besides, I know it's late in the year for you to change schools, but I'm sure Stephen can get you a tutor and arrange it so you can officially finish school, if you

61

want. Are you interested in going to university?"

"Maybe. I've always been interested in psychology, funny enough."

"Well, if anyone can get you there, it's Stephen."

Herman took a bite of her salad and sighed in ecstasy, thinking she could easily get used to living this way.

"Those women asked if you were going to start *another* coven. Did you belong to one before?"

"Stephen and I formed one in university, yes. It only lasted a couple of years. Stephen still practices witchcraft. Me, not so much anymore."

"Stephen's a witch?"

"Yep." Margaret nodded.

"Why didn't you stay in the coven?" Herman wondered how long it would take before the many strange subjects that had come up over the past twenty-four hours would feel like normal topics of conversation.

"It began to get out of hand, as far as Stephen was concerned, and I had to agree."

"In what way?"

"Well, first rumors got out that we were performing sexual rituals that amounted to orgies, and then everyone wanted to join. Even people who had no desire to be a witch."

"And were you? Having orgies?" Herman asked, her eyebrows raised.

"Technically, no. At least not at first. Some of the rituals were sexual in nature. But for most of the time the coven existed, there were five women and only one guy, and that guy happened to be Stephen. One thing led to another and the rituals became more sex than ritual." She shrugged. "We were all young, with nothing to lose."

Herman stopped eating and stared at Margaret.

"Anyway, it didn't take long for Stephen to get tired of it, particularly when all these people wanted in just so they could have sex with him, so we both quit. The coven broke up after that," Margaret said with a wave of her fork.

Herman put hers down. "So, you've had sex with Stephen?"

Margaret looked her in the eye. "I've had sex with Stephen," she said. "There's no point denying it. But that's all it was. Sex. Nothing more."

"Huh." Herman stabbed at a piece of lettuce.

"Stephen is my best friend and he always will be. But he's been looking for love for a long time, and he's never once looked my way to find it."

"Does that bother you?"

"Not at all. I only want him to be happy."

"What have I got myself into?" Herman mumbled, shaking her head.

Margaret reached across the table and touched the young girl's hand with her fingertips. "The chance of a lifetime."

Herman gazed down at her salad and skewered another bite with her fork.

"What are you thinking?"

"I'd really just like to see Stephen again and talk to him," said Herman with a sigh.

Margaret took her cell phone out of her pocket and glanced at it. "Speak of the devil," she said.

She put the phone to her ear and said, "What's up?"

There was a pause. Margaret looked at Herman with a smile.

"Can you give us about an hour?"

Another pause.

"K, bye." She pushed a button on her phone and put it away. "Good news. Stephen wants to see you, too."

"Did he say why?"

"He's building something out at the station, and he wants to try it out."

"Do you think I'll get to see some serious magic?" asked Herman anxiously.

"You'll probably be part of it, in fact. We'd better hurry and eat. 'The Great Dagmaru,'" Margaret raised her hands and wiggled them in the air, "doesn't like to be kept waiting."

CHAPTER 11

Herman and Margaret walked straight through the house, out the kitchen door, and up to the stable where they found Reed waiting with the three black horses. Two were saddled and ready to go.

"Miss Flowers." He bowed to Margaret. "It's nice to see you again."

"And you, Reed. How have you been keeping?"

"Very well, thank you."

"Miss Anderson," he said as he handed Herman the other set of reins. "I trust you slept well last night?"

"Yes, I did, thanks for asking," said Herman, feeling as though she had been put in her place, far above what she was used to.

The three headed out to the station at a comfortable trot, Reed riding bareback. Herman's heart leapt when they rounded the corner and she saw Stephen leaning against the wall on the station's platform, his arms and legs crossed casually.

"It took you long enough," he said with a sly smile.

"You should know better than to try to rush women through lunch," said Margaret as she dismounted expertly. Herman tried to look as graceful, not wanting to be outdone in Stephen's eyes. They were trained only on her.

"Reed," said Stephen. "I'm going to need you inside, too."

"Right away." Reed took the horses to tie them up.

Herman and Margaret followed Stephen into the

station. They went through the old waiting room to the area behind the ticket booth. Standing in the middle of the room, where yesterday there had been nothing, was a wooden ladder, a full two stories high. Held upright by a wooden frame on both sides, it was attached to the ceiling in the dimness above the lights.

"I know it's not very pretty right now, but it'll be dressed up for the show," said Stephen, looking up at it with pride.

He put his arm around Herman, still admiring his work, and said, "So what do you think?"

"It's a ladder," she said steadily, hoping her voice didn't expose the full-body tingling that his touch caused.

"Ah, but it's not *just* a ladder." He smiled at her. "It's a magic ladder. You're not afraid of heights, right?"

"Right."

"Excellent."

"I know better than to ask what it does," said Margaret from behind them.

"We only need to wait for Reed to hold the camera. I want you to watch firsthand what my wonderful new contraption can do."

"And I'm ..."

"Climbing the ladder," Stephen finished the sentence for Herman.

"Oookay," she said. "Is this going to freak me out?" She raised her eyebrows and glanced back and forth from Margaret to Stephen. They answered her at the same time.

"Probably," said Margaret

"Nah," said Stephen.

Reed came in, and Stephen stepped away to retrieve a video camera from the table that was nestled between the two armchairs.

"You know how this works," he said as he handed Reed the camera.

"Yes, Sir."

"Are you ready, Herman?" Stephen asked.

"As I'll ever be, I guess."

"Okay. What I'd like you to do is climb the ladder. Go up this side, so you're facing away from us."

"Just go up?"

"That's it. When you get to the top, you can do a little flourish." He demonstrated, holding out his hand and gracefully curling his wrist.

"And then what?"

"Then come back down."

"That's all?" she asked, waiting for the punchline.

"I have a feeling this is to prove it's just a ladder," said Margaret, crossing her arms. "The real trick is still to come."

"You know me far too well," Stephen said to Margaret, though he didn't look at her. He was still grinning and gazing upon his invention.

"Here goes nothing, then." At the foot of the ladder, Herman grabbed the rung at the level of her face and shook it experimentally. "Feels sturdy," she said over her shoulder.

"Don't worry," said Stephen. "It will hold you."

Herman began climbing, slowly at first, then with more confidence. She made it all the way up, turned the top half of her body to look at her audience far below, and did a flourish with her hand as instructed. Stephen and Margaret clapped and she climbed down.

Stephen met her at the bottom of the ladder.

"Now what?" she asked.

"Now you're going to go around to the other side, so you're facing us." He held her hand as she stepped through the scaffolding, then he spoke to her through the ladder. "When you go up this time, I want you to go slowly and count, in your head, the rungs that your feet step on. Not the ones your hands touch. I'm going to tell you to stop

LINDA G. HILL

when you're about halfway up, and I want you to remember how many rungs you climbed."

"Only the rungs I climb with my feet?"

"Only the rungs your feet touch," he confirmed.

"Got it."

She climbed slowly, counting as she went. He told her to stop on the fifteenth rung. She looked through the ladder at him down below, and asked, "Now what?"

"How coordinated are you?" he called up.

"Pretty well, I think."

"Good. Now I want you to climb upward with your hands, and downward with your feet. Five rungs with each."

"Oh God, no," said Margaret.

"What?" Herman asked her sharply.

"Never mind, dear, just do as he says," answered Margaret in an unnaturally high voice.

"Steady with the camera, Reed," Stephen said to the young man.

"Okay, here it goes." Herman started going up and down at the same time. Concentrating hard on what she was doing, she barely heard Margaret's muffled scream, and Reed's "Holy crap" from behind the camera.

"How do you do this?" Herman asked, without looking down. From her perspective, it felt like the ladder was sliding in on itself, as though it was getting lower at the top and higher at the bottom. Which was impossible, since the ladder was still touching the floor. She completed the five rungs as instructed and looked down to ask Stephen what to do next. What she saw was Margaret sitting with her hand clamped over her mouth, Reed holding up the camera with his mouth hanging open, and Stephen grinning from ear to ear. Herman decided to wait until she got back down to find out what the commotion was.

"Do I climb in the other direction again?"

"Yes," said Stephen. "Up five rungs with your feet and down five with your hands. Count carefully."

"Very carefully," Margaret piped up.

Herman did as she was told. When she completed the five rungs, she asked if she should come down.

"You've done well, my love," Stephen said, smiling. "You can come down now."

Stephen met her at the bottom of the ladder again and helped her through the scaffolding. Herman's heart beat heavily in her throat at hearing Stephen call her "his love." It didn't matter if it was simply a saying he used, it felt wonderful to hear it directed at her. She walked with him to join Reed, who stood staring at the ladder as though it had just fallen out of the sky from another planet.

"Do you want to see the video?" asked Stephen.

"You'd better sit down first," Margaret said to Herman.

Herman sat in the unoccupied chair, and Stephen knelt beside her holding the camera so they could both see it. Margaret leaned over to watch, and Reed stood behind them.

She saw herself go up and down the ladder the first time without incident, then she began her second ascent. True to what she remembered, she stopped at Stephen's command, halfway up, and then they discussed what she was going to do next. When Herman saw herself begin to move again, and she saw the top half of her body come apart from the bottom half, she let out a scream, not muffled by her hand like Margaret's had been. She watched in horror as the two halves of her body got farther and farther apart, her top half climbing effortlessly and the bottom half staying perfectly, impossibly balanced.

"What would have happened if I'd miscounted?" Herman asked Stephen, the sensation in her throat no longer having to do with endearments.

"I'd have come up and helped you," he said calmly.

"Just don't ever miscount," said Margaret as the video version of Herman came back down the ladder in one piece.

Herman snorted. "I didn't feel a thing."

"Can you do it again?" Stephen asked her.

In the smoldering glow of his eyes she saw magic and she saw confidence, and in that moment she knew she trusted him with her life.

"Let's go," she said.

They performed the trick two more times, but with all her focus on her task, Herman didn't have the opportunity to look at Stephen while she was climbing in different directions. She was curious to know what kind of magical feats he performed when she was cut in half, so she asked him if Reed could record Stephen instead of her.

She came down after the fourth time to watch the video. She heard her own voice speaking to Stephen and saw him give his instructions to her, but there was no perceptible difference in him while she was being ripped in half, nor was there any sign of relief when she reached the point of being back together.

"How do you do it?" she asked him. "You're not down here conjuring up spells or waving a wand."

"Oh, I'll have a wand or a cane for the sake of the audience," he said. "Half the magic is the drama, the suspense, and the emotions I draw from people. That's where the real conjuring comes in."

"So, where's the rest of it?" she asked.

"I told you. It's the ladder that is magic."

"I don't believe you."

Stephen smiled and pulled her in to kiss her on the forehead. It was a much friendlier kiss than the one he had blessed her with the night before, but it thrilled her all the same. He held her long enough to say in her ear, "You'll know everything there is to know, soon." She had the feeling he wasn't just talking about the magic trick.

"Well, then," he said. "Would you like to take a break from this and see some of my older tricks?"

Exhausted by the intense concentration, Herman said yes. Stephen dismissed Reed, asking him to return one of the saddled horses to the stable. He pulled a folding chair from the corner and sat opposite Herman and Margaret around the small table. In finest magician form, Stephen made a new deck of cards appear.

"All this, and card tricks, too?" Herman exclaimed jokingly.

"I know after the ladder it's not much. But what respectable prestidigitator doesn't know how to do card tricks?"

"Presti-*what*?"

"Prestidigitator. One who performs sleights of hand."

Stephen broke the seal on the deck and shuffled. "Unless I'm performing up close or for kids, I rarely do card tricks."

"Do you have special adult-oriented tricks? Ones that aren't fit for a general audience?"

She was surprised when he said, "There have been a few."

Margaret smiled. "You wouldn't get away with those performances anywhere in this country."

"Where did you do them?"

"Japan," Stephen and Margaret said at the same time.

Stephen shifted to the edge of his chair and asked Herman to watch closely. He held the deck of cards horizontally in one hand, directly above the other. He fanned them quickly from his top hand down to the bottom one. When she looked down to the bottom hand, the deck was there, back in its package. The package was sealed like new.

Herman laughed. "That's amazing."

He unsealed, then opened the deck and took them out

to show her. The cards were shuffled.

"New cards are in order," she said.

Stephen smiled. "They're not new. You just saw me shuffle them."

"But ..."

"But he's good," said Margaret. "And I think you're going to enjoy yourself here." She patted Herman on the knee. "And speaking of being here," she said to Stephen, "do you want me at the house, doing anything for you?"

"Actually, you can be of more help here, if that's okay. Are there things you need to take care of this afternoon?"

"Nothing that can't wait. I'm at your complete disposal today."

"Great. I'd like you to help me demonstrate some more tricks. It's much easier if Herman can watch before she tries them herself."

"Before we get into anything else, does this place have a ladies' room?" Herman asked.

"Of course," said Margaret. "Go out to the waiting room and turn right, past the ticket booth. It's on the other side."

"Thanks," said Herman, and she hurried out.

"I thought you wanted me to keep her away until dinner," Margaret said as soon as the young girl was out of earshot.

"I know." Stephen chewed a fingernail. "I'm having a harder time with all this than I expected to."

"No one said it was going to be easy," said Margaret. "You know Herman's a virgin, don't you?"

"I had a feeling. What makes you so sure?"

"I could tell by the way she reacted when I told her you and I'd had sex."

"Fantastic," he said with a sarcastic laugh. "How can I do this if I'm going to have any hope of a relationship with her? How can I even begin to expect her to understand?"

"You don't have a choice. You wouldn't be going through hell right now if you didn't care about her. She wants to be with you, too."

He raked his fingers through his jet-black hair. "I know. Just don't leave me alone with her for too long. I can't get into something serious with her until this is all resolved. It wouldn't be fair."

"Don't worry. I'll keep an eye on you both."

Not far away came the sound of water rushing through pipes. Margaret and Stephen sat in silence, waiting for Herman to return.

***

Stephen spent the next few hours teaching Herman some of his more complicated tricks, with glittering props and structures, all of which he had conceptualized and built himself. With the help of Margaret, who had seen them done hundreds of times, the younger girl learned a few tricks to do on her own and how to assist him in some of the others. She also watched Stephen perform more magic that couldn't be explained. He froze boiling water in an instant and produced a bird from behind his back. For the grand finale, he put Margaret into a box that was almost the size of a small room and closed the door. He turned to Herman, smiled at her, blew her a kiss, and then opened the door of the box. Margaret was still there but she wasn't alone. Standing in the box with her was one of the black horses they had ridden to the station on.

"Are you ready to go back to the house?" he asked Herman.

"You really are amazing. Now how do you get the horse outside?" Herman looked with dubiousness at the size of the door frame out to the waiting room.

"There's a bigger door at the back." He nodded to Margaret and she led the horse around the box.

"Let's go." He took Herman's hand, fingers entwined, and they went out the way they had come in. Stephen secured the station door and retrieved the other horse that was unsaddled.

"Have you ever ridden double before?"

"No," said Herman, smiling at the thought of sitting close to him. "But I've ridden bareback before."

"So, you've had some experience then."

"A little," she replied with a sudden knot in her chest. *Not nearly enough where you're concerned*, she thought.

He handed her the reins and held out his hands, fingers locked, making a stirrup with them.

"Put your knee in here." As he lifted her up, she swung her other leg over top of the horse. He jumped up behind her. Margaret came around the corner already mounted, and they started off for the stables together.

Herman enjoyed the closeness of Stephen's body against hers; with the rocking of the horse walking beneath them, she closed her eyes in blissful peace. "I could do this for hours," she said quietly.

"We will, soon," he said, close to her ear.

CHAPTER 12

The next morning, a knock on Herman's bedroom door woke her up at precisely seven o'clock. She'd been left alone for a few hours the evening before while Margaret and Stephen went out to make arrangements for an upcoming show. Stephen had shown up in time to accompany her to the guest room door. He apologized for his absence and blessed her with another kiss on her forehead. She had then watched as he descended the stairs to his office, leaving her wondering if he ever stopped working.

She threw her new pink silk robe on over her new black silk pajamas and opened the door. The man in question stood on the other side, holding a breakfast tray laden with food, juice, coffee, and a bud vase with a single pink rose.

"Room service, *Mademoiselle*?"

Returning Stephen's bright smile, she let him in and raked her hand through her hair self-consciously. "Bed head," she said.

"You look beautiful this morning," he announced, placing the tray on the bed.

Herman moved to close the door but he stopped her. "Better leave that open. I don't want anyone who comes to check on you to think I'm doing anything untoward."

"Ah yes, we must maintain my reputation as a lady," she said with a grin. "How did you know what I like?" She sat near the pillows and looked hungrily at the tray.

"I didn't. I brought you everything *I* like, so whatever

you don't eat, I can have."

"Ha! I like everything. You just might starve, unless I take pity on you and let you have some."

"I'd be honored to simply watch you eat."

She laughed. "I'm kidding, go ahead. There's no way I can eat all this."

"Good, I'm hungry." He picked up a slice of buttered toast and sat on the end of the bed.

"So, what is first on today's agenda?" She chose a muffin.

"We're going to Brockville, to pick up the stallions."

"Back to the scene of the crime. You're not going to put me on the train with my backpack and tell me this was all just a dream, are you?"

"Not a chance," he said, shaking his head.

"Good." She nibbled thoughtfully on her muffin. "I want to call home and talk to my brother before we go."

"There's a phone in my office. Help yourself."

"Having a picnic without me?" said a voice from the doorway.

"See?" said Stephen. "I told you someone would be around to check up on you."

"Well, Margaret," said Herman," you'll be pleased to learn that my virtue is still intact."

"Er, good, I think."

"Inside joke," said Stephen.

"Right," said Margaret. "I forgot to mention last night, I got a call from a friend of ours. Mark Standish. You remember him?"

"Of course." To Herman he said, "Mark had a huge crush on Margaret when we were in university." He turned back to his friend. "What did he want?"

"Mark heard you were in town, and he wants you to do a private show for him."

"He knew I was home already? News travels fast."

Stephen sipped his coffee.

Margaret went on. "Mark has a birthday party coming up for Tracey, his seven-year-old daughter, and he asked if there was any way you might be free. For an old friend."

"Did you say yes on my behalf?"

"No, I said I'd talk to you first. But I do think it would be a good idea for Herman to get her feet wet, so to speak. Easy kids' tricks, small audience."

"Small, yes," said Stephen. "The small ones can be the most brutal." Stephen turned to Herman, "By small I mean the kids, not the size of the crowd."

"Oh, that's okay," said Herman. "I'm great with kids. I practically raised my little brother."

"Well then," Stephen said to Margaret, "call him and say yes. We'll start rehearsing some children's tricks tomorrow."

Herman put her muffin down. "Can we start this afternoon?"

"I have things I need to take care of this afternoon," Stephen said, glancing down at his hands.

"So you're going to hang out with me," said Margaret, animatedly.

"Oh." Herman had a feeling she was being passed off.

"There are certain things I need to do that I can only do alone," Stephen said.

"I understand," said Herman, brushing off her disappointment.

Margaret changed the subject. "I saw Reed and Hawkins hooking up the trailer out by the barn about fifteen minutes ago. Shall I go and get you a Thermos of coffee for the road?"

"I can do that," said Stephen, getting up. "We'll let Herman finish her breakfast and get dressed in peace."

"Okay," said Margaret. "See you later, Herman."

Stephen blew Herman a kiss as he followed Margaret

out the door.

Half an hour later, she met Stephen in the foyer downstairs. He held a flask under one arm, two covered mugs in one hand, and Herman's jacket, which he held up for her, in the other.

"Everything okay at home?" he asked.

"Yep. Chad's handling it like a pro. He promised me he'll be fine until Dad gets home."

Outside, Reed waited in the passenger seat of a midnight-blue pick-up truck with a matching horse trailer attached. Both sported an insignia, which was a golden dagger and a crescent moon. The dagger had an ornate figure of a gargoyle for a handle; the blade sliced through the bottom portion of the moon. Written below it was "Dagmar Farms" in gold cursive script. Reed got out so Herman could slide over to the middle, and Stephen climbed into the driver's seat. He tuned the radio to K-Rock as he pulled out of the driveway.

Along the way, gradually relaxing in the company of the two men while they discussed whether the black horses would go on tour with Stephen, Herman wondered at the logic of taking the truck and trailer to Brockville.

"If you're a magician, why did we have to drive to get the stallions?" she asked with a smile. "Couldn't you just have magicked them home?"

Stephen laughed. "And what if they needed to take a poop on the way? I'd hate to think where it might have landed."

Herman giggled at the image in her head. "I wonder if it's considered as lucky to have a horse poop on your head as it is for a bird to do it?"

"I don't think I'd feel very lucky," said Stephen.

A little more than an hour from the time they left Kingston, they slowed and turned into a long, oak-lined laneway with a small parking lot at the end. Stephen backed the trailer expertly through the large doorway of a barn that resembled the one at the Dagmar estate. A man in jeans and cowboy boots with a face that was cragged like a cedar fence rail met the trailer at the door. He held up a hand when it reached the right spot inside.

"Nice to see you again, Mr. Dagmar," the man said, approaching the truck. Stephen stepped out and rolled up his shirtsleeves as he strolled over to shake the man's hand.

"And you, Pete."

"Reed." Pete nodded in Reed's direction over the truck bed.

He turned back to Stephen. "Thank you for coming to get the horses yourself."

"Did they perform well for you?"

"Sure did," he said, glancing into the depths of the barn where Herman saw a teenage girl leading a sleek dark horse toward them. "We have six mares in foal thanks to your boys."

"Let me know if you actually get six foals out of it," said Stephen. "Let's get them on, Reed."

Herman followed Stephen to the back of the trailer. The girl was inside, tying up the horse she had led in.

"Jake was the easy one," she said.

With a wave of his hand, Pete said, "Okay, Reed and I will get Mojo."

As she passed Stephen, Herman watched the girl do a double take as profound as the one he had executed when he met her on the train. Stephen smiled and the young girl blushed deeply. She headed toward a stall filled with supplies, her head down.

"Didn't you say a bum rope worked with this one, Reed?" she called as she walked.

"Yeah, Bev," he called back.

Bev returned, carrying a coiled rope. She tied one end to a loop on the rear of the trailer, and Stephen climbed into the trailer to wait. Reed came from the other end of the barn leading the beast by two ropes and a bucket of oats. The moment the horse became aware of the trailer, it started backing up. Reed hopped into the trailer and handed Stephen one of the lead ropes. Together they pulled, but the horse refused to go on; the whites of his eyes showed as he began to panic.

"Hurry up," Reed called to Pete and Bev.

Herman stood back to watch, intrigued, wondering how they were going to manipulate the unwilling animal. As Stephen and Reed continued to hold the stallion's head steady from inside the trailer, Bev threw the longer rope around the back of the horse to Pete, who threaded it through a loop on his side. Bev joined him and together they pulled. With the rope tucked against the horse's buttocks, they essentially pushed the animal while keeping well out of danger. After five minutes of clashing of wills, the humans won. The stomping, snorting stallion stood in the trailer, and Stephen and Reed jumped out of a small escape door at the front. They wiped their brows in such a similar fashion, that once again Herman glimpsed the resemblance. Reed closed the trailer's back door on the side of the calmer horse. As he shut the second door, Mojo kicked it out of his hand, almost knocking Bev off her feet as she walked past.

She threw the ungrateful animal an extra half a bale of hay through the side door and patted Reed on the arm as he passed her to go to the front of the truck to get in.

"Good job," she said to him.

"You too," he replied, smiling at her.

Herman stayed behind the trailer with Stephen and the two employees of the farm while they said their goodbyes.

Pete shook Stephen's hand again. "It's been a pleasure."

"Thanks very much for your help," Stephen said.

He turned and nodded to Bev. She waved to him

awkwardly, blushed, and tore her gaze away from his face, in that order. As she hurried away, she called, "Bye, Reed," over her shoulder and disappeared into the dark recesses of the barn with the rope.

"That was fun, wasn't it?" Stephen ushered Herman to the driver's side of the truck and opened the door for her to get in.

"Exciting!" she said as he turned the key.

"You must come out this way a lot," Herman said to Reed. "They seem to know you pretty well."

"I went to school in Brockville. I know lots of people here."

"Haven't you always lived at the house? I assumed since you're there every day, you must live at least close by."

"I do, now," said Reed. He looked out the passenger window as though he didn't want to say any more.

"The Currys live on a parcel of land on the east side of the property," Stephen explained to her. "Reed lives there with his parents and Nina."

The explanation left Herman feeling like she was prying. She changed the subject.

"Do all the girls react to you that way?" she asked Stephen as they started down the highway.

"What way?"

"Oh, come on. She couldn't keep her eyes off you. And when you spoke to her, I thought she was going to keel over."

"Ah-ha. You mean the same way you acted when you met me? I see what you're talking about."

"I did not!"

He smiled at her, briefly taking his eyes off the road.

"Okay, maybe I did a little bit," she admitted.

"Does that answer your question then?"

"I suppose," she sighed.

She turned the radio on in time to catch the middle of "Bohemian Rhapsody." Together they head-banged, *Wayne's World*-style.

***

When they arrived home, Stephen backed the trailer into the barn. Herman slipped out the driver's door of the truck behind him as he and Reed debated the best way to get the horses out.

"I think if we take Jake out first," said Stephen, "Mojo's going to get upset about being left in there alone."

Reed disagreed. "With all due respect, he's quiet, right now. Maybe we should just give it a try."

"Okay, open the door to Jake's half and see how Mojo takes it."

Reed opened the door on the left side, and as Stephen predicted, Mojo gave a mighty kick that bent the door outward on his side of the trailer.

"Shall I get in by Mojo's head and unfasten him, Sir?" Reed asked with a jolting degree of respect that Herman wasn't sure she would ever get used to.

Stephen said yes and instructed Herman to stand way back while Reed got himself ready. She hurried to the opposite side of the barn to watch.

Stephen stood beside the trailer door and released the top and bottom latches. The moment the door opened, the panicked animal charged out in reverse. Free of the trailer, it screamed and flailed across the barn, legs flying in all directions, dragging Reed along with him directly toward Herman. She backed up until she could go no farther. Pressed against the door of a stall, she reached around and tried to work the latch. It was hopeless. The horse was too close. She squeezed her eyes tightly closed and waited for the pain, knowing in the next second she was going to die, crushed between horseflesh and wood. It was the last thing she knew.

CHAPTER 13

Stephen stood off to the side and watched the horse right itself. Stunned at having run into something solid, the animal calmed, snorting but no longer frenzied.

"Shit," he said under his breath.

"Where did you put Miss Anderson?" Reed asked him, unfazed.

"She's up at the house. Can you handle things out here?"

Reed let out a deep breath. "Yes, Sir."

Stephen set off at a run. He entered the house through the back door, climbed the stairs and went into the office part of his bedroom. Margaret sat at the computer desk just inside the door, tapping her foot.

"Hi," she said, taking off her headphones.

He hurried past her without a word and up three steps to the curtain that separated his bedroom from the office. Lacking anything else solid, he knocked on the wall. "Herman? Are you okay?"

"I ... think so ..." came a timid voice from the other side.

"Can I come in?"

He heard the rustling of sheets and then, "Okay."

"Do you want me to go?" Margaret asked quietly.

"No, stay there, please," he answered and slipped past the curtain and into his room.

Herman sat on his king-sized bed with the covers

pulled up to her chin. "What happened? The last thing I remember, I was about to be crushed to death by a horse. Then I woke up here."

"Ah, yeah. About that," he said, trying not to smile. "I guess I owe you an explanation. May I sit?"

"It's your bed, I think."

"Yes, it is." He sat a respectful distance from her.

"You're not just a garden-variety magician, are you?"

"No, I'm not. I transported you here using real magic."

"Ah-ha," she breathed, her eyes searching his.

"I've only been in the position a few times where I've had to save someone from something horrible happening to them. After one awful incident, when I moved someone out of danger to somewhere even worse, I trained myself to move people to the safest place I could imagine them to be. It's imagining a place—envisioning it in my head—that is where they'll end up. I only had a split second to remove you from the barn, and all morning I've been thinking about having you here, like this." He looked away, smiling to himself.

On the other side of the curtain, Margaret cleared her throat.

"Where are my clothes?" asked Herman, her face still half hidden under the sheets. Her eyes were smiling.

Stephen looked around the floor of his room. "I have no idea," he confessed, laughing self-consciously. "I'll get you some more, shall I?" Without waiting for an answer, he went through the hidden door to the right of the bed.

***

"There *is* a door there," Herman whispered to herself. "I knew it."

She looked around the room. It was decorated much like the one across the hall except it had a darker color scheme. The walls were a deep green, but the furniture was a lighter shade of wood. She hugged her knees and thought about what Stephen had said about having her in his bed. Was it possible that she had finally met someone who wouldn't be scared away by her, as they inexplicably had in the past? Excited at the prospect, she screamed a little into the sheet she held up to her face.

Stephen reappeared with a quick knock on the wall, her robe draped over his arm.

He placed the garment on the bed where she could reach it. Gathering her courage before he could step away and driven by her desire, she rose to her knees, holding the sheet in front of her. She seized the back of his neck with her free hand and kissed him on the lips. Relief flooded her when he responded, tasting her tongue with his, gently and yet insistently. He held her close, wrapping his arms around her, careful not to touch her bare skin with his hands. Her eyes were closed and her ears rang and her breath came heavily. Every part of him that she touched seemed electrified, surrounding her, as though his entire spirit enclosed her in its embrace. She would have allowed it to go further if Margaret hadn't called Stephen's name from the curtain, where she stood watching.

They turned at the same time.

"I'm sorry to interrupt; you're needed downstairs."

He waited until Herman had a grip on the sheet to hold it in front of her before he moved away.

"I'm sorry," he said. "Get dressed, and I'll see you downstairs."

Herman sat back and sighed. For a first kiss—in fact the first in her experience that hadn't ended in the guy running away seconds after their lips met—it was magical.

***

Stephen nodded to Margaret on his way out the door. Halfway down the main staircase, he sat and raked his hands through his hair. Taking a deep breath he looked up, surprised to see that there was, indeed, someone at the door. He thought Margaret had interrupted the kiss because of his request to help see that he didn't get carried away with Herman.

"Hello," he said.

An old woman with shadowy gray hair stood, stooped over the black patent-leather handbag that hung from her arm. Her light-rust-colored raincoat and ankle boots gave the impression that she had somehow arrived directly from the eighties. Her heavy eyes brightened as Stephen approached her. He held out a hand in greeting, but she didn't take it.

"How can I help you?" he asked.

"I'm Herman's great-aunt. George's mother's sister."

"It's nice to meet you. Won't you come in? I'm sure Herman would love to see you …"

"Just take good care of her, prick." Her voice sharp, she looked him directly in the eye. "Don't fuck her around." With that she disappeared as though she had never been there.

Feeling ridiculous but unable to resist, he opened the door to see if there was any sign of her. There wasn't. With a shake of his head, he retreated to the kitchen. He plopped himself into a chair at the butcher-block table and rested his head on his arms, listening to the activity of the kitchen staff. When he felt a hand on his arm, he looked up to behold Herman, dressed again and smiling at him.

"What's wrong?" she asked, seeing his expression. "You look like you've seen a ghost."

"I think I have. A foul-mouthed one who said she was related to you."

Herman's eyes widened. "You saw Aunt Aggie?"

"You know her?"

"She used to sing me to sleep when I was little. She's

been in the family, as a ghost, for years. But no one outside of my dad's family has ever seen her. Not even my mother. It makes sense. She's always been around when I was in danger. It was probably the horse incident that woke her up."

He squinted. "Didn't she know I saved you?"

"She was probably just checking in." Herman smiled. "She must think you're special."

"Yes, well, she scared the hell out of me." He rested his head on his arms again. "You can let her know next time you see her that I'm not."

"I think you are," Herman whispered in his ear, kissing him lightly on the lobe.

"I'm starved. What's to eat?" Margaret sang as she waltzed in the kitchen door.

"Wow, your timing is great today," Herman said in jest.

"Why, thank you."

"I'm not sure I have an appetite," said Stephen, lifting his head once again.

"Poor dear has had a hard day already, and it's only lunch time," said Herman, patting him on the shoulder.

Nina came in from the outer door and hung up her jacket on a hook.

Stephen put his head back down, mumbling into his arms, "And it keeps getting better and better."

"There's a pile of clothes outside," said Nina to no one in particular.

Herman let out a snort of amusement and clapped her hand over her mouth.

"I'll look after those, Nina," said Margaret. "Where did you leave them?"

"They're just outside the door, Miss Flowers."

"Oh good," murmured Stephen, low enough that only Herman could hear. "I was afraid they'd been sucked up the horse's ass."

Herman burst with laughter and put her hand affectionately on his arm.

He stood and took Herman's clothes from Margaret when she came back in. "I have to go upstairs anyway." He sniffed them warily so he could enjoy the sound of Herman's laugh again. He gave her a quick kiss on the lips and left them to their meal, knowing three sets of eyes watched him leave the room.

***

Herman and Margaret ate a casual lunch at the table in the kitchen. No Nina meant Herman was happy. She assumed since they weren't eating in the dining room, the servant had better things to do. When they finished, Margaret asked Herman if she wanted to see the rest of the house.

"I think the only thing I haven't seen is the playroom, isn't it?" Herman asked.

"And you're not going up there until Stephen takes you there himself. By the time you get there, I'll have moved out."

"What's up there? I was imagining a Playstation or a Wii ..."

"Ah, no. The playroom is more adult-oriented than that. And since you're not officially an adult yet, I'm not going to be the one to introduce you to it. Besides, if you wait until Stephen takes you up there, you'll thank me for not ruining it for you."

"It's not some sort of torture chamber, is it?"

Margaret shook her head. Her eyes smiled as she said, "Far from it."

"What else haven't I seen, then?"

"How about the bath room?"

"You mean the washroom?"

"No," said Margaret, "the bath room. It's beside the

downstairs office. Come with me."

Herman looked up the stairs as they passed them, hoping to catch a glimpse of Stephen, though she didn't really expect to. With Margaret leading, they entered the living room and stopped facing a bookcase that covered the entire wall, with multi-colored, hard- and soft-cover volumes. Margaret reached just above her head to pull out a thick, black fabric-covered book that bore a golden shamrock on its spine. A door-shaped section of the bookcase fell back and slid off to one side.

"What mansion would be complete without a secret passageway?" she asked, smiling at Herman.

Herman followed her through the new doorway.

"This," Margaret said, holding up the book, "is the key. If you lose this particular book, no one can get in. And make sure you bring the book in with you. If someone puts it back in place, you won't be able to get out unless you break a window. The room is soundproof, so no one will hear you scream." Margaret's eyes widened in mock fear, then she laughed. "Just kidding. But it is soundproof."

She turned, then, and pressed a button on the wall; the door closed so that only a fine outline showed. The room was long and narrow. A glass wall to the right had a door to a greenhouse full of tropical flowers, matching wicker chairs and table, and an Oriental stone lantern. The three remaining walls and the floor were covered in an unpolished red-brick-colored ceramic tile. The rear wall also had a window.

Along the long inner wall stood a wooden wardrobe, stained to a tint close to the hue of the tiles. A low wooden stool sat below a removable showerhead, and a wooden bathtub, large enough for at least two, nestled below the window at a level to allow its occupant to gaze outside while bathing.

"Wow," Herman sighed. "I've never seen anything like

it."

"It's a traditional Japanese bath room. Stephen was so impressed with the ones he visited in Japan that he had one built here. The bath is always full of warm water. Everyone uses the same water. You shower first with soap and shampoo, and rinse off," she pointed to the showerhead and the stool, "and then you soak in the bath."

"It's beautiful."

"You can use it if you'd like. Any time. Personally, I love it. I used them whenever I had a chance when I was in Japan with Stephen. It took a while to get used to the communal ones, though. This one is made for one or two people. In Japan, you can stay in places where they specify only the women or only the men use them at any given time, but there are others where you'll get in the bath and a strange man will show up and get in with you."

Herman looked at her wide-eyed.

"Naked?"

"Yep," said Margaret. "They do things differently over there."

"Do you think Stephen will ever go back there?"

"I know he'd like to," said Margaret. "It's such a beautiful country. And the people are wonderful."

"But strange."

"But different. Do you want to try this out now?"

"Do you have anything else for me to see?"

"There's probably only the aviary you haven't seen. Do you like birds?"

"Yes. What kind?"

"Doves," said Margaret. "The staple of a magician's trade."

"Right." She rolled her eyes at herself.

Margaret silently waited for her decision.

"You know what? I think I *will* have a bath. It's nice and calm in here, and it'll give me a chance to get my mind wrapped around everything that's happened in the last couple of days."

Margaret smiled. "Good idea. You'll find robes and slippers in here." She opened the wardrobe where half a dozen identical plush white terry robes hung. Identical slippers, with neither lefts nor rights, were lined up below. "And the windows are tinted from the outside, so you don't have to worry about privacy.

"Just come out when you've finished. I'll be in the living room on the laptop." Margaret put the book on the top of the wardrobe. "I'll leave you with that." She pushed the button to open the bookcase and left Herman alone.

CHAPTER 14

Herman emerged fresh and clean and warm from her bath an hour later. She found Margaret and Stephen sitting on the sofa together before the large television screen, watching a movie that she recognized right away.

"Pirates!" she exclaimed with a smile.

At the sound of her voice the two friends turned.

"It's a lot cooler out here than it is in there," she said, reaching up to replace the book that would close the door.

"Come and sit here," Stephen said, patting the spot to his right on the sofa. "I'll keep you warm."

"I thought you were busy this afternoon." She sat and curled her bare feet underneath the bottom of her robe and snuggled up to him.

"I finished doing what I needed to and thought I'd come and find you." He put his arm around her and she did feel instantly warmer. She wondered briefly if it was part of his magic but decided she didn't care. She only wanted to be close to him. He offered to pause the movie so she could get dressed but she declined, saying she was too comfortable.

They laughed together at the funny parts and groaned at the more gross parts. Herman couldn't remember having enjoyed the movie more during any of the past dozen times she'd watched it with her brother.

When it ended, Margaret picked the remote up off the table in front of them and clicked off the TV.

"I was telling Margaret about my encounter with your Aunt Aggie," said Stephen. "We both wondered if it was your father who conjured her up. If that's the case, then he might be using her to look for you."

"You think she might not be just the family ghost?"

"It's quite possible that she is," Stephen said. "But at the same time, your dad might be able to use her to keep you safe and to keep tabs on you."

"Wait, are you telling me not only is my dad a magician, but that he's like you? That he actually has powers?"

Stephen nodded, yes.

Herman took a moment to organize the information in her head. "Do you think my dad knows where I am?"

"That's one thought. We'll know if he comes knocking at the door."

"I wonder why he never told us." Herman looked across the room, staring at nothing.

"I have a theory." He took her hand in his. "Your father doesn't actually play the part of the magician onstage. His boss, Paul Whitmore does that."

"What does my dad do?"

"He's a magician's assistant."

"A male assistant? You don't see that often …" Herman gasped, realization dawning. She sat up to face him. "He's not a guy onstage, is he."

"No. He— She goes by the name of Mona Lisa."

"Shit!" she said under her breath. "I've never told anyone before …" She looked into Stephen's eyes and hesitated over the words she was about to utter.

"I saw my dad once when he didn't know I was home sick from school. I walked in on him while he was sitting at my mother's mirror putting makeup on. And he was wearing a dress. He made me promise I'd never tell anyone.

"Why does he do it? Why isn't he just a magician?"

"Maybe it's lack of confidence," said Stephen. "Who knows? I haven't been able to figure it out."

"But you figured out that he has real powers, though."

Stephen nodded. "I've seen them do tricks that there's no way Paul could actually have been performing. The closer I watched them, the more I came to realize that it was your dad, not Paul, who had the talent."

"He can't be a very convincing woman."

"Actually, he is. I think part of his magic is being able to turn himself into one. I wouldn't have known he was a man if I hadn't met him after a show."

Herman frowned then, contemplating a much harder question.

"Do you think he's gay?"

Stephen shook his head. "No, I don't believe so."

"I always thought he was gone all the time because he was screwing around on my mother. I guess it was more complicated than that." Herman watched distractedly as Margaret got up and walked away from the sofa. "It's really weird. I had to come so far to find things out about myself."

"I've found the same thing," said Stephen. "Sometimes you have to leave home to discover what you're all about."

"But you came back home," she said. "Does that mean I'll have to go back home?"

"Not until you're ready."

"And what if my dad does show up at the door?"

"Then you'll have to decide what you want to do." Stephen squeezed her hand gently. "I'll stand behind you if you want to stay," he looked down at their hands, "or I'll support you if you choose to go."

She leaned forward and he kissed her gently, his hand on her cheek.

"There was another thing I needed to talk to you about," he said. He swiveled to face her, not letting go of her hand.

"What's that?"

"I have to go away for a few days."

Her heart sank, creating what felt like a lead weight in her stomach. "A few?"

"Three."

"What am I going to do without you?"

"Well, Margaret will be here. The two of you can go out. And you can go riding with Reed if you'd like."

"I'm going to miss you."

"I'll miss you too," he said with a small squint.

"Do you really have to go?"

"Yes."

She turned and leaned back against him. He curled his arms around her again, and she could feel already the emptiness of not having him there. She wondered at the attachment she felt so quickly.

"When the summer comes, I'd like us to go camping," he said. "On the island."

"Sounds wonderful."

"I used to go there with my dad when I was little. That's where he showed me how to do magic."

"Is your dad a magician too?"

"He's never performed onstage. He has the gift of real magic, but he doesn't use it often. He goes through life in a practical way."

"How does that work? He doesn't think about it so it just doesn't happen for him?"

"Something like that, yes."

"But he could if he wanted to?"

"Yes," said Stephen.

"What was the first thing you ever did that was magical?"

"I got mad at my sister and I stole her teddy bear out of her arms." Herman could hear the smile in his voice as he spoke. "I was in *so* much trouble. My mother didn't approve

LINDA G. HILL

of me doing anything by magic."

"Did she feel the same way about your father's magic?"

She felt him nod. "That's one of the reasons he didn't practice it, I think. He is completely dedicated to my mother."

"He sounds like a good role model."

Stephen nodded silently. After a few breaths, he said, "My dad's the best."

"How old were you and your sister when you took her teddy bear?"

"I was nine, so Daphne would have been about four."

"She's the same age as I am, then?"

"Yes," he said. "You're two months older than her."

"When's your birthday?"

"In January."

They were silent for a while. Herman thought about his family. About how it would feel to know the people she loved would be around forever—or at least where she could always find them and talk to them—and not change.

Eventually, she asked, "Why do both you and your dad have magical powers?"

"They run in the family."

"Does your sister have it? The magic?"

"The girls in the family don't have it, as a rule. My dad is working on getting some of our family history translated, but he believes his great-grandmother was the only exception. He found some old documents in the attic in Antigua when he moved there. The house has been in the family for centuries. Anyway, if Daphne does have it, she's never tried to cultivate it."

"But you did …"

"I was fascinated by it. At first, I saw it as a way to get what I wanted. But I had to learn delicacy. It's kind of like being strong. If you're strong and you don't pay attention to what you're doing with your power, you can cause destruction. Like squeezing an egg too tight. It didn't take me long to realize, though, that it wasn't the be-all and end-all to being happy."

"There are some things you can't get by using money and magic, are there?"

"Love, for one," he said, squeezing her tighter.

"Will I get to meet your family one day?"

"Only if we go to them. They haven't been back to Canada since they moved four years ago."

"Antigua must be a nice place to live."

"The house they live in was originally built in the seventeenth century by our ancestors who migrated there from Europe."

"Wow. It's interesting that you know so much about your background. I've never talked much about mine with my parents. But I haven't had much of a chance. Now I may never get one."

"Well, you never know. I'm sure we'll catch up with your dad eventually."

With a sudden thought, she tilted her head to look up at him. "You said your powers run in the family. Do you think maybe my dad's do, too? Do you think maybe I have hidden magical powers?"

He shrugged. "Perhaps. If we see him next year at the conference, maybe he'll give you some answers."

The last several dozen times she'd spoken to her father, he'd been drunk. Now that she'd discovered he was a cross-dressing magician, the kinds of answers she might get were too much to contemplate.

CHAPTER 15

He lies on her bed, on his back — or in her dream it is her bed; she has never seen the room before. There are large windows at the head and to one side of the double bed, as though on the inside of a cottage porch. It is dark outside. She begs him not leave her.

"I'm here now, Herman. I won't leave you."

But you're really here?

He feels insubstantial.

"Yes, and I will stay."

I love you.

"I like being with you. I won't leave."

She lies beside him she kisses him and he kisses her and he feels solid and she believes him that he is there and he smiles and he fades away. A misty figure, a face outside the window wanting to get in and she is alone, afraid. People coming and going that she knows, but she doesn't know who they are.

He is back, lying on the bed and he is smiling and he is beautiful and perfect and she thinks he must be an angel because he is too perfect to be human. She lies down with him immediately. You're here.

"I am with you, and I will stay."

She looks down and there are brussels sprouts on his pants at his crotch. What are these?

"They are my balls."

But there is only one.

"There are three." *He laughs and he kisses her and she climbs on top of him and she kisses him and he holds her and he kisses her and she can feel the love, the all-consuming, all-encompassing,*

98

perfect love that he has for her and she begs him to stay.

"I'll never leave you," he whispers.

And he is gone.

Faces, misty, white faces of ghosts in the window, and she wakes up afraid.

Herman opened her eyes and peered into the darkness, wondering where she was. The digital numbers on the clock glowed 3:15. Stephen's house. She sighed and tried to burrow deeper under the covers, but it was no good. Shaken by her nightmare, which held a confusing amount of love within it, she craved comfort.

She slid her feet into the bath room slippers, shrugged on her robe, and went into the hall. Hoping she had the right spot, she knocked on the wall right across from her door. When there was no answer, she descended to the landing and opened the door to Stephen's office. In the pitch black of the room, she could feel that no one was there. She crossed to the curtain and slipped past it into his bedroom. It, too, was empty.

He'd told her he planned to leave early in the morning when he said goodnight, but she hadn't imagined he meant this early. She hurried downstairs to see if there was any sign of him. She checked the kitchen first, then the dining room. Nothing. She crossed to the living room next. Before she reached the door, she heard a rustling from the sofa. It had been turned to face the fireplace. She wondered briefly why he might be downstairs in the dark. However, it wasn't Stephen she found on the sofa. Covered from the waist down with a blanket, Nina was naked from the waist up, at least. Herman's gasp was enough to rouse the girl from her sleep. She hurried to cover herself, looking as confused as Herman had felt upon waking up.

"I'm sorry, Miss Anderson," Nina said as she ran her hand through her hair.

"What are you doing?"

"I must have fallen asleep."

Herman remembered her own earlier trip, by way of magic, from the barn to Stephen's bed. "How did you get here?" she asked with no small amount of suspicion.

"When I can't sleep I— I sometimes come here. Master doesn't know. Please don't say anything."

Herman snorted and stomped out of the room. Too annoyed to check any of the other rooms, she headed back up the stairs for the playroom. There would be no more sleep until she knew what had happened to Stephen, and Margaret was her best chance of finding out. She crept halfway up the spiral steps and called Margaret's name, softly, so as not to scare her. No answer. She ascended a little farther and tried again. She heard nothing. Frustrated, she climbed until her eyes were level with the playroom floor. In the dim moonlight shining through the window, she spied Margaret sleeping on a futon on the floor.

"Margaret!" Herman whispered sharply.

Margaret stirred and rolled onto her side. "Herman?" she asked groggily.

"Yeah, it's me. Where's Stephen?"

"What time is it?" Margaret asked, lifting her head off her pillow.

"It's about 3:30."

"Stephen left at three o'clock. He had a flight to catch."

"Oh. Sorry to wake you up." She turned to go.

"Wait, Herman. What are you doing up?"

"I had a nightmare."

"I'm sorry. Do you want to talk about it?" It sounded like the last thing she wanted to do.

"I'll be fine. Goodnight." She returned to her room, crawled into bed, and lay awake until dawn.

CHAPTER 16

At breakfast, as Herman contemplated telling Margaret about her discovery of Nina the night before, a short, heavy-set woman dressed in full maid's attire bustled in from kitchen.

"Oh, Lotta," Margaret said. "I want to introduce you to Miss Anderson. Herman, this is Lotta Curry."

"I've heard so much about you from Nina and Reed," Lotta told Herman as she placed a tray filled with extra cream, pastries, and a fresh pot of coffee on the table. "It's nice to have Mr. Dagmar home, and having yourself here as well is like having Miss Daphne home too. It's lovely to have young people in the house. It reminds me of the old days when all the family was together!" She stopped, stared at spot on the table, and said, "Oh dear, that won't do," at something Herman couldn't see and scurried back to the kitchen.

Margaret grinned, hiding her smile with her coffee cup. "Wait for it," she said.

"For wh —"

"I was just saying to Hawkins this morning," Lotta was back with a washcloth, "that we need more children in this house. I think it's about time Mr. Dagmar found himself a nice young lady and settled down. And I do wish Miss Daphne would come home. She doesn't belong in some far-flung corner of the world. This place is her birthright, every bit as much as it is Mr. Dagmar's! Well, this isn't getting anything done." She concluded her scrubbing. "Nice to meet you finally, Miss Anderson," she said, and then she was gone, presumably to talk the ears off the rest of the staff in the kitchen.

"Wow," said Herman.

"Yeah."

"Has anyone ever actually spoken to that woman?"

Margaret laughed and shook her head.

"This place seems so empty without Stephen," said Herman after a few moments.

"I agree. I don't think I've ever been here when he hasn't been."

"Thanks for staying for my sake."

"You're more than welcome."

They ate for a while in silence.

"Do you want to tell me about your nightmare last night? Sometimes it helps to talk about it."

"Not really," said Herman. "Still too disturbing. Where did Stephen fly to?"

"New York City."

Herman stared at her. "I think that's where my dad is supposed to be."

"Huh," Margaret said, picking up her coffee cup.

"Do you think Stephen will run into him?"

"He might."

"He won't tell my dad where I am though, will he?"

"It's hard to predict exactly what Stephen's going to do. But I doubt he'd do anything but tell George you're safe and well taken care of. I expect he'll call later. You'll want to talk to him?"

"Definitely," Herman said. She still hadn't decided whether or not to mention Nina's indiscretion to him, but it seemed like there might be plenty to talk about anyway.

***

After a busy afternoon of shopping and schmoozing,

Margaret was drifting off to sleep on the sofa beside Herman when her phone rang, making Herman jump.

"There he is," Margaret mumbled, wondering if the young girl was always a bundle of nerves.

She put the phone to her ear. "Hey there."

"Hi." The single syllable was clipped and tight. "I ran into Herman's dad at the airport bar. He was on his way to Ottawa. Is Herman there?"

"Yes, she's sitting right beside me."

"Okay, after I talk to her, I need you come back on the phone and make an excuse to get out of the room so we can talk privately."

"I'll let you talk to her." She handed the phone over to a visibly edgy Herman.

"Hello?" She listened and then frowned. "And you didn't tell him?" Herman asked.

Margaret didn't hear the answer, but she knew Stephen would say he wanted Herman to tell her father of her whereabouts herself, when she was ready. She doubted that that was the whole truth.

"Yeah, I miss you too," Herman said. "Bye."

Margaret took the phone. She paused for a few seconds and then said, "Sure, I'll go get them." To Herman she said, "I have to go up to Stephen's office to find some paperwork he needs. I won't be long." She climbed the stairs, pretending to talk about business for Herman's sake.

"Okay, I'm in your office alone. What happened with George?" She sat down at his computer, crossed her legs, and plucked at the pleat in the soft cotton fabric of her pants while she listened.

While he awaited his third flight of the day, Stephen had gone into a Kennedy Airport restaurant and spotted the slight, almost womanly figure of George Anderson perched on a bar stool. He wore a tailored suit jacket over a pair of designer jeans. The man knew how to dress if nothing else.

"Hello, George," Stephen said, sliding onto the stool beside him.

"Dagmar. What the fuck are you doing here?" George slurred, lifting his glass and pouring its contents down his throat. His hair was one shade darker than his daughter's long brown locks, and his eyes were hazel green where Herman's were blue, but the shape of them was the same. It was that, Stephen realized, which had caused the first flicker of recognition when he met her.

"Don't you know?"

Stephen ordered a Glenlivet from the bartender and another one of whatever his "friend" was drinking.

"I have time for another quick one," said George, glancing at his watch. "My daughter's gone missing. I have to go home."

"Really? That's too bad."

Stephen raised his eyebrows to make it appear that he'd come up with an idea. "You know, George, I might be able to help you find her."

The older man turned to face him, and Stephen caught a whiff of rum.

"If you were to do something for me in return, of course," Stephen continued.

"Such as?" George's curiosity made an appearance through his semi-stupor.

"Remember when we met for the first time, in Japan?"

George smiled, searching his empty glass for more. "How could I forget?"

"Well then, how about you tell me what my Japanese assistant gave you, in the way of information."

"She was a nice piece of ass, wasn't she? I'm sure you tapped that any chance you got."

"Now, George, whether or not either of us fucked her is irrelevant. What I want to know is what she gave you of a non-sexual nature."

"And what makes you think I should? How can you help me find my daughter?"

"I have my ways." The bartender came with their drinks, and Stephen placed a twenty on the bar. "Just like you had ways of getting things out of Yuka that she probably didn't even know she knew."

"You give me too much credit, Dagmar."

"And you don't give me enough."

George looked at him, straight-faced. "You're just a kid with a bunch of magic tricks. Why don't you keep hiring new assistants to fuck, and leave the real magic to me, okay?"

Stephen laughed. "Fine by me." He knocked back his drink and walked out of the bar.

"What an ass," said Margaret, after hearing Stephen's story. "I guess he didn't get any tips from Aunt Aggie after all."

"Nope, guess not," said Stephen. "And not only that. If he doesn't know I have any genuine powers, then he probably didn't find out as much as I thought he had from Yuka."

"True enough," she said. "So, where are you now?"

"I'm still in Ottawa."

"Are you heading out to the island right away?"

"I don't have much choice. I can't stay away, even for a day."

"Do you want me to send Nina out there ahead of you? To get things ready?"

"Is that what we're calling it these days?"

"I'm sure the place is dusty," said Margaret, not wanting to address the real issue. "I doubt anyone's been out there in a while. And if you're sleeping there for the next couple of nights, you'll need the place put in order."

"True," said Stephen. "Go ahead and send her."

"How about me? Are you going to need me for

anything else for the next couple of days?"

"If I do, I'll call you," he said. "Just stay with Herman."

"I might be taking her places then. I've got work to do if you want to do any shows in the near future."

"Please keep her safe for me."

"Don't worry, Prince Charming. Your Princess is safe with me."

They said goodbye, and Margaret went downstairs to ask Hawkins to get a boat ready, to take his daughter out to the island and leave her there. Then, she returned to Herman, to let her know they would be going for a drive after dinner. Margaret was happy to distract Herman, but not more than she was pleased to have a reason not to ponder the plight of her best friend, and what he would be doing on the island.

CHAPTER 17

After another full day of running around town, Margaret and Herman arrived home just before dinner. Margaret had wanted to eat out, but the book Herman had read the night before convinced the girl that she needed to spend time with the rabbits they'd purchased for the children's show. Margaret left her to it and headed to the playroom to get a change of clothes for a bath in the Japanese tub.

She climbed the spiral staircase to the rhythm of a steady drip of water dropping into what should have been a dry Jacuzzi with a sense of dread that chilled her to her toes. Her blood pressure rose a notch when she found Nina in the tub, dozing off. Margaret knelt beside the bath and whispered in Nina's ear, "Having fun?"

The servant woke up with a start, sloshing water over the sides.

"What the fuck are you doing in here?" Margaret hissed.

Nina struggled her way out of the Jacuzzi. "I came to get supplies and—"

"And you thought you'd take advantage?" Margaret shot back. "I don't know who you think you are, but I can tell you right now there is no way in hell your 'Master' is going to put up with this. Now get the fuck out. And don't *ever* come up those stairs again."

"I'm sure Stephen won't mind, now that—"

"Now that what, Nina? Now that Stephen is having sex

with you just to make a baby? He *has* to, Nina. He has no choice. I know you know that somewhere in your addled brain. It's not romance. It's sex, plain and simple. And how dare you use his given name? Even you know how dangerous that is!

"You're delusional. Get out."

Nina hurried down the stairs still dripping. Margaret heard her getting dressed at the foot of the staircase. She felt a tiny pang of sympathy for the girl, but it was essential that she be taught a lesson, and this seemed the only way. Margaret wanted to get in touch with Stephen immediately, but it probably wouldn't help if he was angry at Nina. He still had to get the servant pregnant, preferably before Herman's eighteenth birthday. And without Herman finding out.

CHAPTER 18

Mid-morning the next day, Margaret was working at the kitchen table when Stephen called wanting to know where Herman was.

"She's in her room reading. I have strict instructions to let her know the moment you get home, bless her."

"Okay, I'm coming in the kitchen door," he said.

"Hello." Margaret hung up as Stephen walked in, followed closely by Nina. "You'd better get her out of here," she said, nodding in the young woman's direction. "She's glowing."

Nina smiled and Margaret scowled at her.

Stephen turned to his servant. "You can go home. Don't come back until late tonight."

"Yes, Master," she said and turned to leave. Her head was down, but Margaret could see that she was still smiling to herself.

"Come and talk to me before I see Herman?" Stephen requested as the door closed.

"Sure, let's go into the downstairs office."

Stephen shut the door behind them. He pulled the chair out from the computer desk, and Margaret sank into an armchair in the opposite corner of the room, facing him.

"How are you holding up?"

"Where do I start?" he replied, resting his elbows on his knees and raking his fingers through his hair. "Well," he continued, "Nina told me about the playroom."

"She *told* you? She's got more balls than I expected her

to have."

"She was trying to get some emotion out of me. Anger is better than nothing."

"I'm guessing you didn't buy into it?"

"I did my best to keep my temper. I tried to explain to her how stupid she was to do such a thing and that she might be putting us all at risk by simply acting as though she isn't a servant." He shook his head. "But I don't know if anything gets through to her. She's in her own world. Sometimes I wonder if she really believes in the curse."

"She wants you," Margaret sighed.

"And she'll do just about anything to get me."

"This is so fucked up."

Stephen put his head in his hands. "I don't know if I can stand this much longer. Deceiving Herman like this."

"You really love her, don't you?"

He nodded.

"Stephen, you've known all along that the curse couldn't be lifted unless you were in love with someone. That it would come to this eventually."

"Yeah. I talked to my dad after I met Herman and he confirmed it. He found everything when he went through the attic at the house in Antigua. The curse, as it was originally recorded after it was cast, says I can't put an end to it unless I'm unfaithful. But that doesn't make it any easier."

"Nothing will," she said, feeling defeated on her best friend's behalf.

"I want you to watch."

"You want me to *what?*"

"I want you to watch me with Nina," he clarified, looking her in the eye.

"I don't know. I think that might be going a little above and beyond the call."

"Okay, you don't have to watch. But I want you to be

there at least one time, so you can say to Herman with all sincerity that I didn't enjoy it. And that there's absolutely no love in me for Nina."

Margaret crossed her arms over her chest. "It wouldn't be the first time I've been with you when you were with another woman. But doesn't this feel a little shameful?"

"I can't possibly be any more ashamed than I already am. Nina will come to the upstairs office tomorrow afternoon. I'll make sure Herman is busy with Reed, and you can stay and work on the computer while Nina and I are ... doing what we have to."

"I guess I can just be there."

"It never takes long."

They sat silently, each of them lost in thought.

"You should go and see Herman," Margaret said at length.

"I need a shower first." He stood and left the room without looking back. As she reached the door, she saw him disappear into the living room.

Margaret dawdled on her way up the stairs to tell Herman that Stephen was home.

"Where is he?" Herman threw more than dropped her book and sprung off the bed.

"He's downstairs in the bath room having a shower. He'll be out soon ..." Margaret finished the sentence to an empty room. Herman was already halfway down the stairs.

CHAPTER 19

Herman burst into the living room and stopped dead. The bath room door was closed. But of course it was. She plopped herself onto the sofa, resigned to wait. A few minutes later the door slid open. Like an immaculate male sculpture, Stephen stood in the doorway holding a towel around his waist, his hair dripping and his chest and arms covered in beads of unevaporated water. He smiled and held out his free hand to her.

She rushed to him, mouth first, feeling his lips on hers and then his warm body as he crushed her against him with one arm. She stood on her toes wishing she could climb him. Anything to be closer to him. She kissed him hard, and he responded with his teeth on her lips, on her tongue. She wanted to push him back into the bath room and shut the door behind them, knowing no one could disturb them in there. She made a wistful attempt at it but he resisted. He drew away from her lips and smiled again at her.

"Hello," he said.

"Hi." The unprecedented sensations that his body caused in hers made her shiver.

She unwrapped her arms from around his neck and dropped her fingers to his nipples, brushing the hardened tips, only to have her hands gently pushed away.

"Careful," he said. "I'm only human, you know."

"Funny you should say that. I had a dream that you were an angel."

He placed his hand at the back of her neck and pulled her to him again, more insistent than before. He curled his fingers through her hair and bent to kiss her.

"I'm not an angel." His voice was deep, and all at once it occurred to Herman that this was not a boy, but a man she was toying with.

He kissed her again with an urgency that surpassed her playful eagerness to push him into the bath room. He pressed up against her, and she found that not only his nipples were hard. As he held her in his solid embrace, she felt the fire that smoldered deep within him and she became unexpectedly unnerved. Unready. She stiffened and tried to step back, but he held her tighter.

Just as she lifted her hands to push him away, Margaret walked in.

"The cavalry has arrived," he said quietly, easing his grip on her neck. "You don't need to be afraid." There was a sadness in his eyes that mismatched his gentle smile. Her mind returned to her dream, and she felt suddenly lost, unreal, like the world could vanish around her and leave her alone in an instant. Alone without Stephen. *"I'll never leave you."*

She watched his face when he looked up at Margaret; by the time his eyes focused on the woman across the room, both the sadness and the smile were gone. He looked annoyed.

"It took you long enough," he said.

He held Herman at an angle so that her body rested against his hip. She lay her head against his chest and the room seemed to go dark around her. Margaret said something that made him laugh, but Herman didn't hear what she said. She only felt the solidness of him, the warmth, his respiration, and his movement as he laughed. His heartbeat reverberated in her ear like the steady pulse of a clock, yet she wished time could stand still while she stood close to him. She felt as confused as she had upon waking from her dream. Then, as suddenly as it all began, he kissed the top of her head and the atmosphere shifted. Everything returned to normal.

When she looked up at him, he smiled at her with all the parts of his face.

"I can't keep babysitting the two of you if you want me to get any work done," Margaret was saying.

"I think we'll be okay," Stephen said. "Don't you, my love?"

"I think so." Herman's voice shook.

"Why don't you go and get yourself dressed," Margaret said to Stephen.

He guided Herman to the sofa and released her gently from his single-armed embrace. She sat, and he knelt before her and brushed her cheek with his knuckles.

"Are you all right?" He searched her eyes, frowning with worry.

"I'll be okay. Go and get dressed. I need to talk to Margaret."

"I'll be back soon," he said, exchanging a look with his friend.

"Don't worry," Margaret answered.

She sat beside Herman as Stephen left the room.

"Are you going to be okay?"

"I don't know." Herman shook her head, still trying to get clear of the nightmare.

Margaret held her hand. "He scared you, didn't he?"

She nodded, tears forming in her eyes.

"What did he do to scare you?"

"At first I thought it was just because he was so … male. You know? I've never really been with a guy before. I've only had one kiss from a boy. But Stephen …"

"Is a man," Margaret finished for her. "A grown man in full arousal can be startling when you're not expecting it, especially if you've had no experience. And as men go, Stephen is an exceptional one."

Herman silently agreed. She wiped her eyes with the back of her hand. "But that's not all of it. It's that stupid dream I had the other night. It made me feel like there's something I'm not seeing. Crazy, isn't it?" She looked pleadingly at Margaret. "I'm scared I'm going to lose him, or that Stephen's not a real live man in the first place.

"Margaret, I want to be with him. I really do. Maybe I'm just not ready."

"I think that's possible. Do you want me to talk to him for you?"

"I don't know. I feel so stupid," said Herman, sniffing.

"Don't. He'll understand."

"Are you sure?"

"He probably already does."

A warm breeze billowed the curtain, and Herman became aware of the birds twittering outside. Spring was in the air. As she sat with her arms crossed tightly against her body, looking down at her lap, she felt a presence at the door. Out of the corner of her eye she saw Margaret look up. She put her hand on Herman's knee.

"Do you want to see Stephen?" Margaret asked in a low voice.

"Yes and no." Herman looked up and saw Stephen standing in the doorway dressed in jeans and a button-down shirt, a hand on each side of the frame. Worry still darkened his features.

"Yes," said Herman. She waited for him to sit on her other side.

"Do you want me to stay?" Margaret asked her.

Herman felt Stephen nod.

"For a while, please," said Herman.

Eyes focused on her lap, she gathered her strength to speak. Before she could, Stephen did.

"I'm sorry," he said.

"No, I am," said Herman. "I feel silly now." She laughed mirthlessly as she stared at a piece of lint on the carpet. She heard Stephen sigh.

"Herman," he said, leaning toward her. "I have a confession to make."

She turned her head partially. She wasn't ready to look him in the eye yet.

"You know how overwhelmed you were when you arrived? I am as overwhelmed by you."

Herman stared at him then. "By me?"

"By you and by the feelings I have for you. I'm not trying to use that as an excuse for coming on strong before. That was me losing control of myself, and for that I'm sorry. I won't let it happen again."

"It was my fault."

"No," he said firmly. "Don't ever think that."

"What is it that you're overwhelmed about then, if it's not that?"

"Herman—" He sat with his mouth open, trying to get the words out.

Margaret got up and Herman watched her walk out, wondering what was going on. She turned back to Stephen.

"The moment I saw you on the train, I knew there was something special between us. Or at least I hoped so. Now …" He paused and looked deeply into her eyes. "Now, I hope I can say how I feel without scaring you away. Herman, I'm in love with you." His eyes were filled with hope and awe. He seemed not to breathe.

Another soft breeze blew the curtain, and the scent of spring, of life, filled Herman's senses. She felt giddy; she exhaled a short laugh.

"It's okay." He reached for her hand. "You don't have to—"

"I love you too." It poured out of her from deep inside.

Stephen smiled. As tentative as she'd yet seen him, he placed his fingers below her chin and leaned forward to kiss her gently.

When their lips parted, the awe, combined with an inexplicable confusion, remained in his eyes.

"I don't understand," she said. "Why is it so overwhelming for you? You've been in love before."

"Never," he whispered. "I've never felt like this before."

Herman gravitated into his arms.

"Does this mean you're not going to disappear on me?" she asked, clutching him tightly.

"I'll never leave you," he whispered in her ear.

Herman began to cry uncontrollably.

***

Reclining on her bed with her head propped up on pillows, Nina gazed at The Great Dagmaru pictured on the glossy posters that covered the walls of her room. Her Master. In some his arms were raised, some showed his profile as he concentrated on the magic he was performing. She often spent hours just staring at him. And now that his baby was growing inside her, they would be part of each other forever, connected by flesh and blood and the love they would share for their child.

She remembered the night before he went away for a year to the United States, when he had taken her virginity. He had been drinking alone in the living room by the fire, staring at the flames as they licked the blackened wood. She had come to ask him if he needed anything before she went to bed, and he had asked her if she was ready. Just like that. *Are you ready?* She knew at once what he meant. She knelt at his feet and told him that she was. He said he wasn't in much of a relationship, but he still felt that he was in one, in a way. Nina knew he meant that he felt like he would be cheating on her, whoever she was. He asked her if she was afraid, and she told him that she was, a little, even though she wasn't. For years he had made love to her in her dreams; her life was full of him in theory, in anticipation. She had waited all her teenage years for that moment. She was eighteen, and he was home and prepared to give her a child, if they were able to conceive. He told her to take off her clothes. He handed her a blanket and walked away from the sofa to pour himself another glass of wine so she wouldn't feel self-conscious. She did as she was told, then she sat and covered herself. Drink in hand, her Master stood over her, regarding her as though wondering how to proceed. He sat beside her and looked at the fire through his glass, half filled with red liquid.

"This will be my first time," she told him, trying to sound nervous and shy. She wondered if the red wine reminded him of blood. The blood he was bound to spill when he broke her with his love.

"I'll do my best not to hurt you," he said.

He leaned over to kiss her, their one and only kiss to date. When the brief kiss ended, he told her to kneel, facing the sofa. She remembered vividly the sensation of the rug on her knees and the cool, soft leather beneath her bare breasts. He knelt behind her and touched her, making sure she was physically ready for him. He had entered her then, causing her to moan.

"Am I hurting you?" he had asked.

"No."

"Then be quiet please, unless I do."

He continued, going gradually faster, holding her hips. She waited until he began to moan, and she did so again.

"Too much?" he had asked her.

"Not enough," she whispered.

That seemed to excite him more and then he had hurt her, but she refused to make a sound. The passion she had evoked in her Master was more wonderful than she could have anticipated. She wouldn't give it up. By the time he finally released her hips and removed himself from her, she was, indeed, bleeding. He stood and left without a word. The next day he was gone.

The memory of their coupling had sustained her through her first menstruation afterward, and through the next year.

Now he was home. Since the night he returned, they had been together at least once every day. Their time alone on the island was magical in so many ways. She had watched as he sat in a lotus position, meditating and hovering, naked, a foot above the water, fifty feet from the shore. When he wasn't practicing magic, they had sex. Morning, noon, night, and in between. On her bed, against the kitchen counter, outside against the wall, or where ever she was when the mood struck him. He found her and told her to turn around, and then he would take her from behind. Always from behind.

The only thing Nina missed during each of their sexual encounters was the passion that he had presented her with their first time, long ago. So much did she want to get that back, that she provoked him by angering him. She was genuinely afraid when he became enraged because she went into the playroom. But it had worked, at least a little. He took her afterward, thrusting into her harder and more times than could be counted on the fingers of one hand, which he normally didn't do. She couldn't repeat such an act of bold disobedience; she realized after he spoke to her about what she had done that it was, indeed, too risky. But there were other ways to evoke emotion from him. Pity, sadness, and of course the happiness he would feel when she told him that together they had created a new life.

Conception had occurred mere hours ago. She knew it. While her father waited for them at the boat, her Master led her to the servants' house on the pretense of taking one last look around. He had pinned her against the inner wall of the porch on the opposite side of the house to where her father was standing on the dock, and he had impregnated her right there, while she looked out through the screen at the lake.

But it didn't have to be the end. She didn't expect her period for almost two weeks, which meant she still time to enjoy physical and emotional bliss with the love of her life. Her Master. Stephen Dagmar.

***

Stephen had spent the rest of the day trying, without success, to coax an explanation from Herman for why she had broken down in tears after they professed their love for one another. She seemed troubled right up until moments ago, when he said goodnight to her. He walked slowly down the corridor to his upstairs office, wondering if Herman sensed something was going on and knowing who he would find in his spare bed. He stopped at the door and thought about how he desired to make love to Herman the way a woman should be made love to. With respect. He thought about the servant lying naked in his bed, and he knew he could use his resentment for the circumstances to drill Nina to tears. The only person who would gain any satisfaction from it, however, would be Nina. It would leave him more shamed, unhappier, for having been unfaithful to Herman on this, the day he had told her that he loved her and her alone.

Stepping through the door, he made his decision. Nina's gentle breathing turned to a moan as he touched her foot to wake her.

"Go home," he said.

"What? Why, Master?"

"I can't. Not tonight." He slipped through the curtain to his own bed, leaving Nina to dress and leave.

CHAPTER 20

The week leading up to Mark's little girl's birthday party flew by for Herman in a flurry of morning rehearsals and afternoons of horseback riding, relaxing, and visiting the sights of Kingston with Stephen. Her worries about Stephen being less than real had faded, much like most dreams do, as she rediscovered how easy he was to be around.

The afternoon before their dress rehearsal—two days before the performance—she stood on the landing outside the closet, discussing with Stephen what she might wear. She asked him to help her look for an appropriate dress, but he refused, hands raised.

"If I get in there with you, I won't be responsible for my actions. I'll ask Margaret to help. Besides, I have to go out this afternoon."

"Where?"

"*That* is none of your business, young lady," he said with a sly smile.

"And what if I insist on knowing?" She stepped up to him and he put his hands around her waist. Standing on her toes, she took his bottom lip between hers and kissed it.

"I still won't tell you."

"Are you getting mysterious on me?" she asked, narrowing her eyes.

"Yes, it's more fun that way."

"Fine!" She spun away from him. "I can be mysterious too."

"Oh you can, can you?"

"Yes."

"How?"

"I can go and try on dresses without you," she said, shimmying into the closet room and closing the door behind her.

She was flicking through the racks of short and long, sparkly and shiny, bright and dark, and high- and low-cut clothes of every description when Margaret entered about three minutes later.

"Kids like the colorful ones," the older woman suggested.

"Have all of these been worn?" Looking at the sheer number of outfits it seemed unlikely, but then again, Stephen had been performing for two years already.

"Most of them, but not all. Don't worry, they've all been cleaned."

Herman focused on the bright-colored dresses. "Some of them are really gaudy."

"They look that way in here, but they look fantastic onstage with all the lights."

"So, where is Stephen going today?" Herman thought she would slip it in, to see if she could catch Margaret off guard.

"Where did he tell you he was going?"

"He wouldn't."

"Well, then maybe it's a surprise."

"Why do I feel like I'm always left out?"

"Maybe because I always know where Stephen is and what he's doing?" Margaret hypothesized.

"Is that ever going to be me?"

"I certainly hope so. Not that I'm getting tired of being his right-hand gal, but it's about time he had someone other than his agent in his life."

"You're not just his agent, though."

"True, I'm his friend. But there should be someone more important than me." Margaret turned to face Herman with a shocking-pink, fully sequined dress in hand. "And I'm in agreement with Stephen that that person should be you."

"When?"

"Soon enough. I told you right from the beginning you'd have to be patient."

"*Hmph*," said Herman, taking the dress from her. She took off her t-shirt and jeans to try it on.

"You have better bras and panties than that, don't you?"

"Not really."

"I think we need to go shopping again."

She tried on four outfits, all of which fit perfectly. Since the party was for a little girl, they agreed the pink one would be best.

"Does Stephen like all of these dresses?" asked Herman while she pulled her jeans on and Margaret returned the show clothes to their hangers.

"He bought them all himself. I'm thinking he probably does."

"Did he enjoy looking at them on his other assistants?"

"If you're asking me if you should be jealous, the answer is no. Stephen wasn't in love with any of his assistants. Before now, that is."

"But he still found them attractive," Herman prodded.

"Yes, he did."

"Did he have affairs with them?"

Margaret looked up at the ceiling and exhaled. "Okay, Herman, listen. Stephen has had what you might call a colorful past. He had no one to answer to, nothing to lose, and the world was his oyster."

"So that would be a yes, then."

"But, what's important is that now he is ready to settle

down. Now he does feel as though he has someone to answer to, that person being you. You needn't be worried about what he's done in the past. Concern yourself with the future."

"Did he have long-term relationships with them, or were they more one-night-stands?"

"Damn it, Herman, you're like a Rottweiler. Once you have something in your grip ... Yes, Stephen had long-standing relationships with both of his past assistants. But they're long gone."

"Thank you," said Herman. She gazed at the rack. "I just wish I had a dress of my own."

"Sweetie, give it time. You'll have everything your heart desires."

Margaret finished hanging up the clothes and turned to face Herman. "I think you and I should go out tonight."

"What about Stephen?"

"He'll be okay on his own."

Margaret grabbed a black dress off the rack.

"You're going to wear this. I'll do your hair and makeup, and you are going to find out what it's like to live."

"What do you mean, 'live'?"

"Herman, you've been sheltered. You've never exposed all that beauty of yours. You keep it hidden. You need to know how it feels to be seen, particularly so you'll be able to understand what it's like for Stephen when you do finally go out together in public. People react to him differently than they do most people."

"I've noticed. There was this girl at the farm where we picked up the stallions. She was perfectly normal talking to the other guy there and to Reed, but the second she saw Stephen she started blushing, she couldn't speak; she became a virtual bowl of jelly."

"Yeah, that happens a lot around him." Margaret

looked at her watch. "It's four o'clock now. You grab a shower, I'm going to let Stephen know, and then we'll get ready. Dinner and then dancing."

"I don't suppose I have any say in the matter."

"What would you rather do, hang around here for another night? No," Margaret answered before Herman could. "You need this, and I need it too. Maybe I can meet someone. It's been way too long."

***

Margaret caught Stephen just before he ducked out the front door. "I'm taking Herman out to meet guys," she said as she descended the stairs.

Stephen laughed, "No you're not."

"Not for her, for me."

"Fine, but you're only allowed to bring one home," he said. "But seriously, what are you up to?"

"I'm getting us both dolled up, and we're going out dancing. Before *you* take out her anywhere nice, she needs to know what it's like to have the opposite sex go gaga over her. Otherwise, she's forever going to feel insecure when she's with you."

"Okay, fair enough. I'll take Nina back out to the island one last time. I've cast enough fertility spells all over it to ensure triplets. If that doesn't work —"

"Let's not even go there," Margaret interrupted.

"Anyway, she's expecting her period tomorrow, so this is my last chance."

"You know how slim the chances are of getting her pregnant the day before her period, right?"

"Of course. But I'm desperate. What time will you come home? I want to be here when you do."

"I'll have Herman home by two, Dad," she teased.

"Intact."

"Of course."

Stephen huffed out a mirthless laugh and bit his nail.

"It'll all be over soon," Margaret reassured him. "Then you and Herman can have each other all to yourselves."

"If she stays. I'm trying to figure out how I can convince her that I can fuck Nina and not feel anything."

"It's not going to be easy. It takes experience to really understand that there's a difference between sex and making love."

"Hopefully she'll let me show her."

"When will you give Herman her surprise?" asked Margaret, changing the subject.

"I'm going out to get it now. I'll give it to her tomorrow. I'm going to take her for a long ride out by the water."

"That will be romantic." Margaret sighed. "Oh Stephen, every woman needs a man like you."

"I wonder if you wouldn't all be better off without a man like me," he said as he turned to go.

CHAPTER 21

The wind lashed at the branches, threatening to pull off the early leaves with an impending storm, as Stephen pulled up to the Curry residence. He rang the bell, his coat whipping around his legs in the dark.

"Oh, Mr. Dagmar, to what do we owe this pleasure?" Lotta asked, offering to let him in with a sweep of her arm.

"I require Nina tonight. Now, if possible."

"Right away, Sir. I'll go and get her."

In less than a minute Nina appeared, alone. She took her coat from a hook beside the door and slipped on her shoes without a word. Together, they went out into the night.

"We're going to the island," he told her.

"In this?"

He gave her a hard look.

"I'm sorry, Master," she said, her head lowered. "I shouldn't question you."

It began to rain the moment Stephen slipped behind the wheel of the truck; by the time they arrived at the boat launch, it was coming down in sheets. The wind gusted, and the water chopped and churned. Stephen thought briefly about transporting them both to the island by magic, but if there was any chance Nina was already pregnant, he might risk her miscarrying. The stress the process took on the body was something he didn't fully understand. At the same time, he knew the small motorboat wouldn't make it to the island without magic. He helped Nina in and told her to hang on tight and keep her head down. He cranked the engine, turned toward the island and hit the throttle. The rain stung his face, and the boat flew, barely touching the tips of the waves. When they reached the dock, Stephen swung the back of the boat around so they faced the mainland. He hopped out and reached out to take Nina's trembling hand.

"Are you okay?" he shouted over the wind.

"I'm cold."

He nodded and led her by the hand to the smaller of the island's two houses.

Safely out of the rain, Stephen took in the sight of Nina, soaked through and shivering. "Would you like some tea?"

"Certainly, Master," she said. She moved toward the kitchen.

"Sit. I'll be right back." He left her in the living room, breathing on her hands. A few minutes later he returned carrying a cup of Japanese green tea for her and a glass of Johnnie Walker for himself. He crossed to the fireplace and built a teepee of kindling in the grate. Fingers splayed, he moved his hand above the wood and it burst into flames.

"Master, may I ask you a question?"

"Yes."

"Will you send our baby away, like your father did with Reed?"

"No. I want to raise him or her myself. We will share custody."

Nina muffled a cry and cleared her throat. "Does that mean, with all due respect, that our child will inherit the Dagmar fortune?"

"Part of it. When my parents are gone it will be split three ways, between Daphne, myself, and Reed. When the three of us are gone, all of our children will inherit it."

Nina gawked.

"Didn't you know Reed would inherit anything?"

"No."

"He may only be my half-brother, but my dad loves him. He won't let him go without, any more than I would let my child with you go without."

"Thank you, Master." Nina stifled a sob and sipped her tea.

"But the only way Reed and our child can inherit anything is if the curse is broken. Please get yourself ready." He returned to the kitchen, draining his glass as he left.

When he came out five minutes later, Nina was on the sofa covered from the waist down with a blanket. He stood in the doorway of the kitchen and looked at her in the firelight. He had expected to get it over and done with quickly, as he usually did, but he was rooted to the spot.

"Stand up," he demanded of her.

She did, holding the blanket in front of her.

"Drop the blanket."

She hesitated only for a second and then did as she was told. He studied her, standing naked and shivering with what could have been either cold or nerves.

"Turn around and face the other way," he said. He crossed the room and stood beside her.

"Now bend over, please."

She placed her hands on the back of the sofa and bent at the waist. He rested his left hand in the middle of her back and inserted two fingers of his right hand inside her, as a doctor might during a pelvic examination.

"You're already pregnant," he said, removing his fingers.

Grabbing his coat, he walked to the door and opened it to the driving rain.

"I'll send your father for you in the morning," he said as he turned and left.

He didn't know whether to be elated or enraged. He was happy that he would no longer be forced into having sex with Nina, and ecstatic that he had created a new life, despite the fact that the mother of his child was not the woman he wished it could be. But he thought if he could tell with only a glance that Nina was pregnant, they had probably not conceived that morning. He cursed himself for not paying more attention.

Now he had the task of telling Herman ahead of him. It would have to wait until the time was right. Preferably not until after her birthday, which was still four days away.

***

Stephen sat on the stairs at the stroke of one, a tumbler of whiskey in his hand, to wait for the girls' arrival home from their night on the town. They stumbled in the front door at half past, both quite drunk.

"Hey look, Dad waited up for us," said Margaret with a giggle, and Herman bent double in a fit of laughter.

Stephen grinned. "Please tell me you weren't out in public like this."

"Nah." Margaret kicked her shoes off. "We broke into your stash of booze in the car."

Herman staggered to the foot of the staircase and looked up at Stephen. He held out his arms and she climbed onto his lap.

"You're beautiful," she said, her voice muffled by his shirt.

"So are you, my love." He looked over her head at Margaret. "You had fun?"

"Balls of fun," she said, which set Herman off again.

"We danced the night away." Margaret tiptoed toward the stairs.

"With plenty of male admirers I take it."

"Scads." She sat on the step beside Stephen's feet and rubbed his calf. "Why don't you take your girlfriend to bed. I think she could use some sleep."

"Yes," mumbled Herman. "Take me to bed."

"Are you staying up for a while?" Stephen asked Margaret.

"Only long enough to make sure you come out of Herman's room."

Herman tittered. "Okay, Mom!" She lifted her head and opened her eyes long enough to glare at Margaret, then she rested against Stephen again, smiling contentedly.

"Let's go." He carried her, cradled in his arms, up the stairs to her bedroom door where he placed her gently on her feet. She leaned on him heavily as he walked her to the bedside to turn on the lamp and pull back the covers. He ran his hand up her spine and down her side, past her waist and over her hip, making her wiggle.

"What you doin'?"

"I'm making sure you're wearing a bra and panties before I help you out of your dress."

"That's okay, I can get those off, too."

"Not tonight, my darling," he whispered in her ear as he tugged down the zipper on the back of her dress. He slipped it off her shoulders and let it drop to the floor, and then eased her down onto the bed. He smiled when he saw what she still wore: a black lace garter belt and black silk stockings, and a white cotton bra and panties with tiny pink flowers. She murmured something unintelligible and fell asleep. Sitting beside her, he tenderly unclasped and then unrolled her stockings and threw them onto the chair in the corner, leaving the garter where it was. He covered her with her heavy down comforter and leaned over to kiss her gently on the cheek, breathing, "I love you," as he stood.

Margaret wasn't right outside as he expected her to be. He found her sitting where he had left her, her body twisted, her head resting on her arm on the step above.

"Don't tell me I'm going to have to carry you upstairs, too," he said, sitting beside her.

She opened one eye and looked at him. "I can make it."

"Do you want to sleep in the office tonight? Save you going all the way up to the playroom."

"No Nina tonight?"

"I left her on the island with no way to get home," he said. "And besides, it's finished."

Margaret sat up abruptly then. "She's pregnant?"

Stephen nodded, unable to keep grin from his face.

"Congratulations," Margaret said, smiling back tentatively. "You're going to be a daddy."

"Yes, and it's finally over with Nina."

"Which means you can be with Herman without feeling guilty anymore. But how did you find out she's pregnant? I thought you took her out to the island to make her that way."

"I figured it out tonight. She *looked* different. Then I felt inside her, and I could feel it—the new life. I don't need a test to prove it. I know it's there."

"Just like you did when you told Charlotte that she was pregnant before she knew," said Margaret, referring to his last assistant, who Stephen had left when he realized she was having her ex-husband's baby.

"Exactly."

"Do you want me to take her to the hospital tomorrow for a blood test? They might be able to detect it, so you can be absolutely sure."

"Thanks, I think I'll take you up on that." He looked down at his hands and the smile fell away from his face. "I dread telling Herman."

"You'll find a way," she said, patting his hand.

"She looked so beautiful and so innocent up there in her little girl underclothes."

"I know. She's about to grow up in a hurry. But I know you." Margaret lowered her head to make him look at her instead of his hands. "If there's anyone in the world who can make this bearable for her, it's you."

"I hope so," he said.

"How did your evening go?" he asked, to change the subject.

"It was nice. Herman got a hell of a lot of attention, and she handled it well. She learns fast."

"So she held all the rabid, drooling creatures off?"

"You really don't have much faith in your own gender, do you?"

"I'm a man Margaret. I know how we think."

Margaret laughed. "Yes, Herman handled the 'creatures,' as you call them, well. I think she may actually be ready to go out with the likes of you. Meaning you, in particular."

"Well, on that note, I think I'll go upstairs."

"Me too."

Stephen stood and helped Margaret up.

"Will you sleep in the office?"

"Nah, I'll go up to the playroom."

They climbed the stairs together. Stephen stopped at his hidden bedroom door and watched Margaret go up the spiral staircase. Rather than heading to his own room, he returned to Herman's. Leaving the door open a crack, he sat in the chair facing the bed and saw her safe until the sun came up.

CHAPTER 22

On the morning of the dress rehearsal, with the sun peeking from between fluffy white clouds, Herman, Margaret, and Reed rode out to the station to meet Stephen. Herman had had all of two hours from the time she woke up to recover from her first hangover; it dissipated much like last night's storm with the anticipation of Stephen's embrace, should she have another chance to ride double with him on the way home.

While Reed tied up the horses, the two women walked into the back room behind the ticket office to find it transformed. As they entered, the lights came on; spots lit the periphery of the floor in red, blue, and yellow. Stephen stepped into a white spotlight in the middle of the room, and Herman's hand shot up to her mouth as she gasped. He wore a black tuxedo with a full-length, full-skirted coat and top hat, and a whiter than white shirt with a lace ruffle down the front and long lace cuffs. Swinging a silver-tipped cane in his right hand, he strolled across the room with his eyes focused on her as though only she existed. He stopped before her, tipped his hat with the end of his cane, and winked at her. Then he took her hand away from her mouth and kissed it.

"Milady," he said looking up at her through his eyelashes, his mouth still hovering over her hand. "Would you do me the honor of being my partner?"

Herman nodded, mute.

She felt Margaret's hand on her shoulder, but the gaze

between the magician and his assistant remained fixed. Margaret whispered in her ear, "Come with me, we'll get you changed." She grabbed Herman by the waist with both hands and pulled her until, finally, Stephen waved to her and she returned to her senses. She turned then and followed Margaret out past the ticket office and around the corner to the restroom.

"Why didn't you tell me he would look that gorgeous?" Herman squeaked.

"What, and ruin the surprise for you? And besides, how do you describe something like that?" Margaret cocked her thumb over her shoulder in the direction of the back room.

"Impossible."

"Precisely." She handed Herman a black sequined dress and said, "Here, put this on."

Herman changed, and Margaret put her hair up with clips and brushed up her makeup. Then she stood back to admire her.

"You look every bit as good as he does."

"Impossible," Herman said again.

"I bet you Stephen will think so."

"Nothing else matters."

As they walked out the door, Herman looked down at herself. "If this is for the kids' party, why am I wearing black? I thought you said kids like colors."

"Wait until you see it under the lights. You'll look like the inside of a rainbow. And besides, Stephen bought it yesterday just for you."

Herman smiled widely at the thought that she had been on his mind, even when they weren't together.

When they returned to the back room, Stephen was standing in the middle of the floor with his feet shoulder-width apart. Both hands rested on top of the cane, which was resting on the floor in front of him, and his eyes were closed. Herman stepped into the spotlight, and he opened his eyes. His face mirrored what had run through her mind when she first walked in.

"My beauty." He dazzled her with his smile and reached for her hand. Lifting it above her head, he twirled her in a circle.

"Herman, you are stunning."

She beamed in response. "Thank you so much for the dress." Looking down at herself, she saw that it did, indeed, sparkle in every color imaginable.

"You're welcome. Let's get started, shall we?"

With Reed recording, they began the performance. Herman started out a little shy, but she soon warmed up to the idea that she could act naturally, even in front of a small audience. The show consisted of the rabbits coming out of a hat, flowers and handkerchiefs of all colors, large rings of gold and silver, and a box from which Herman would disappear and reappear, which was the grand finale. Stephen's twists on all the old tricks were imaginative, entertaining, and funny. Margaret's only criticism was that it started out a bit stiff.

"My fault, sorry," said Herman.

"It's your first time. I thought you did very well overall, under the circumstances," Margaret told her. "But it wasn't just you. Neither of you could keep from staring at each other." She glared at Stephen.

"Why don't we run through it again?" he suggested, laughing.

So they did. The second time was much better.

The three sat down to discuss what could be improved, while Reed went out to re-saddle two of the horses.

"All right," Stephen said to Herman. "You go and get changed, and I'll watch the video. We'll do it one more time at home tonight. Gerald is coming to dinner, so he can be our final critic before the real show tomorrow."

"Okay. But can I do one thing while we're both still in costume?"

"What's that?"

She sat on his lap and kissed him deeply. "Just that," she answered, wiping a smudge of lipstick off his upper lip.

Margaret got up and walked toward the door.

"Go and get changed," Stephen said to her quietly. He patted her bum when she stood, making her squeal. He was laughing softly as she left the room.

***

Out of makeup and back into her jeans, Herman hurried out to the waiting room to find Stephen. He was wearing jeans as well, waiting on one of the long benches with his back to her. As she approached he stood, and they crossed to the window together to wave goodbye to Margaret and Reed, already on their horses and walking away.

"We can take the long way home, if you'd like," he breathed into her hair.

"*Mmmhmm,*" Herman murmured, thinking it was about time they spent some time alone together. Once outside, they mounted the remaining black mare, bareback. Stephen enclosed her in his arms and turned the horse in the direction of the water. They wandered off the beaten path between the trees; the loam under the horse's hooves squished with excess water, bringing the smell of spring to Herman's nose. The sun shone hazily through a thin layer of clouds, lifting the moisture that remained in the ground. Stephen pulled the horse to a stop in the middle of a field of green grass.

"Did you do this with all your assistants?" It sounded jealous but she needed reassurance that his feelings were as strong for her as hers were for him.

He rested his chin on her shoulder. "I've never been on

a horse with one, if that's what you mean."

"Margaret told me you had affairs with them."

"I did. But neither of them meant near as much to me as you do."

"Why? I mean, why not?"

"Because."

She thought he was going to leave it there, but he continued.

"They were both beautiful and talented, and I cared about them, but I wasn't in love with them."

"You used them because they were beautiful?"

"No, not at all. I had great respect for them. The feeling was mutual, though. We had fun together and we enjoyed each other's company, but that's all there was. It was always bound to end. There was no future."

"So, what makes it different with me?" she asked, hoping she knew the answer.

"What makes it different with you is that I can't even imagine a future without you. A future without you is desolate."

She leaned against him, and he tightened his arms around her. She felt a hardness against her, too far up her back to be the horse's spine. This time she didn't mind. He brushed her hair away from her neck and kissed her there, gently.

"You're not a vampire, are you?" she asked with a smile.

"I wish I was right now," he said between kissing and biting her softly. "You taste so good ..."

She put her lips to his and felt his breath meld with hers.

"Forget about my other assistants. I'm with you now. That's all that matters."

"Okay," she whispered.

He nudged the horse's flanks with his heels, and they

resumed their walk until they reached the rocky edge of the water. The sun peeked out from behind the clouds and shone on the water's gentle waves.

Stephen pointed. "Do you see the island out there?"

Herman's eyes followed his finger, but she was distracted by something sparkling brilliantly in his hand.

"What's that?" She drew his hand closer.

"Oh that? It's your birthday present."

"But it's not my birthday for another three days." She took the sparkling thing from him and gasped, "Oh my God, it's beautiful!" She stared at the diamond and sapphire tennis bracelet in her hand. "I've never seen anything so beautiful before in my life!"

"Diamonds and sapphires are your traditional birthstones. The diamond represents enduring love, and the sapphire is for sincerity and faithfulness." His voice wavered a little at the end of his explanation. She tore her gaze away from the jewels to look at him and he smiled. "Happy birthday, my love."

"Thank you so much!" She turned as much as she was able on the horse and kissed him, feeling dizzy with happiness.

"Are you sure this is really happening to me?" she whispered.

"It really is. And I know precisely how you feel." He smiled. "Here, try it on." He took the bracelet and fastened it with its delicate clasp onto her wrist.

"Thank you," she repeated. "I'll never be able to give you anything—"

He interrupted her words with a finger to her lips. "Corny as it might sound, you already give me more than anything you could buy in a store. As long as you're by my side, I'll never ask for anything else."

As the horse walked home beneath them, she ran her hands down his forearms to his hands, which rested on the

139

animal's mane in front of her.

"I'd like to take you on a real date after the show."

"Seems a bit redundant, since we already live together," she said, tipping her head back so that it rested on his shoulder.

He laughed. "You make it sound like we're an old, married couple already. We've only known each other for a week and a half."

"It's been two weeks, three days, and six hours. Not that I'm counting or anything."

She turned her head and kissed him on the lips. He lifted his hand and rested it lightly on her cheek, and they lingered that way, eyes closed, lips just touching, at the mercy of the rocking of the horse's pace.

"I have to behave myself," he said, swallowing, their lips still close. "Until you turn eighteen."

"I won't tell if you don't."

"I've waited all my life for you. I can wait another few days. And so can you. Besides, I could already be in enough trouble for kidnapping you while you're still in school, let alone taking advantage of you in my position of power as your employer."

"I'd rather be your girlfriend than your employee. But," she turned and looked between the ears of the horse, but remained leaning against Stephen, "if we can't enjoy each other yet, we may as well enjoy the ride."

"Oh, I am," he whispered into her ear.

"I can tell," she said, snuggling into him.

***

Stephen and Herman hurried through the bustle of the staff in the kitchen's pleasant aroma of roasting beef, and up the stairs. They stopped at his office door.

"I'm going to take a shower," he said. She put her arms around him and stood on her toes to kiss him, making him squirm. "Make that a cold shower."

She laughed and said, "Me too," as she turned on her heel to climb the rest of the stairs.

He watched her disappear around the corner, wishing the next few days were over and they could begin their happily ever after.

When he opened his office door, he found Margaret at the computer.

"Did you get the pregnancy test done?" The task he'd set out for her first thing that morning had been on his mind all day; he hadn't had a chance out at the station to ask her about it.

"Once they finally brought her back from the island, yeah. Apparently, Nina was so upset she was immovable. According to her, it's where 'my Master got me with child.' Lotta had to be boated out there to get her to come back."

"Well that answers that question," said Stephen. "She knew all along. But I thought she'd be happy to be pregnant."

Margaret rolled her eyes. "Oh, it's not about that. She's happy to be carrying your child. She's just miserable because it's over.

"Anyway, it *is* over." Margaret stood to hug him. "It's official. You're going to be a daddy. Congratulations."

"Thank you," he said, giving Margaret a brief squeeze.

"Now, I'm going for a cold shower."

Margaret smiled and he headed through the curtain to his room.

He popped his head back in a second later. "Where is Nina now?"

"She should be downstairs helping with dinner. She's serving tonight."

"Shit," he hissed under his breath as he closed the curtain again.

He undressed and was about to turn on the tap when

he heard a light knock on the wall outside his bedroom. He wrapped a towel around his waist and opened the door to find Herman.

"Oh!" she said, seeing him half naked. "Sorry, I was wondering what time dinner is and how I should dress for it ..." Her last word was somewhat lost as her eyes ran down the length of his body, stopping at the thin line of hair that ran downward from his bellybutton.

"I was thinking about just wearing towels for dinner tonight," he said, grinning.

Her gaze shot back up to his eyes, and her cheeks turned a charming shade of pink.

"Sorry," she said again, trying on a smile of her own.

He placed one finger under her chin and tipped her head up at the same time he bent to kiss her.

"Stop apologizing," he said. "You have your costume for tomorrow in your room?"

"Yes."

"You don't have to wear it. Go into the wardrobe and pick something. Anything you'd like. I'm going to wear a regular suit."

"Okay." He could tell she was forcing herself to look at his face. She swallowed hard.

"Dinner is at seven," he said, his smile widening.

"Okay," she repeated.

"Do you have a towel for your shower?" he asked. "Because you can have this one ..." He dropped his hand to the towel at his waist.

She blushed immediately. "*No!* I mean, yes, I have a towel."

Stephen laughed. "I know, I'm teasing you."

"You are so bad!" She slapped his arm and turned to go.

"Bye," he said, wiggling his fingers at her as he closed the door.

CHAPTER 23

Nina was having a hard time concentrating. She could tell everyone in the kitchen was getting annoyed with her, but they didn't dare say anything. Did everyone know already that she was pregnant with Master's baby? She still couldn't believe it herself. But there, that was the problem. Every time she thought about it, she got in someone's way. She wished she could just ask them, *Do you know?* She had one close friend among the kitchen staff, but Patsy wouldn't be around until minutes before dinner.

She wondered how long it was going to take before Master told the bitch, Herman. Nina didn't think he would wait until their baby was born. When the bitch found out, she'd leave and maybe Master would ask *her* to be his assistant. She could travel with him and serve him on the road as well as she could at home, and they wouldn't need Miss Margaret anymore. Nina would take care of him better than she could. And when they returned home, they could live together out on the island where they had conceived their baby. Yes, living on the island with him was a fantasy, but she had hope. There was always hope.

She turned from the drawer with a handful of cutlery and walked into one of the kitchen girls, causing her to drop a stack of bowls. Apologizing, she bent to help pick up the pieces but the cook had had enough. She was sent to sit down and wait for the dinner to be ready.

At the big kitchen table, she idly rolled up the corner of

a napkin. She wished her mother was around. Lotta would understand what she was going through. She, too, had been pregnant with *her* Master's baby, a long time ago. Nina didn't think her mother had been in love the way Nina was with Master: her mother had had a husband to turn to, after all. But Nina knew there was a certain amount of affection that went both ways between Lotta and Tarmien Dagmar. Nina's mother hoped the same could be true for her and her Master. She had told Nina about how Tarmien had been there when Reed was born, and how he held him in his arms and wondered at the perfection of the baby they had created together. She told Nina about how Tarmien had kissed them both, mother and child, and had made sure to see Reed almost every day until he sent him away to Brockville. But Master had said he would not send their child away. Therefore, they could be a family, could they not? Nina, unlike her mother, had no husband.

She unrolled the napkin and began re-rolling it. So far, Master hadn't shown her much in the way of affection, but Nina knew she could change that. How could he see her with his seed blooming inside her and not feel pride and affection for her? How could he not feel as sentimental about the time they spent together trying to conceive as she felt? Nina would show him how much he meant to her by her actions in caring for her pregnancy and herself, and by her carefully chosen words and gestures when she was with him. She would show him how sensitive she could be, and that, in turn, would show him how much she would care for their child after he or she was born.

She wondered what Master would want to name the baby. She would love for him to be called Stephen if it was a boy, so she could openly say his name. But of course she would be able to say Master's name once they were together. And they would be together. She knew it. After the baby was born she would have a hysterectomy, and then she would be free from being his servant and free to marry him. In the meantime, she was happy to think of him as her Master. She smiled to herself. He was the Master of her womb and her heart.

***

At six o'clock the doorbell rang, and Stephen came out of his office dressed in a black suit with a white shirt and a sapphire-colored tie. He was halfway down the stairs when Nina came out of the kitchen, headed for the front door.

"Where's your father?" Stephen asked.

She looked up, surprised to see him. "Oh, I—I'm not sure, Master. I heard the doorbell and ..."

Just then, Hawkins appeared from the living room. "You can go, Nina," he snapped at his daughter.

Stephen watched her wander back toward the kitchen as though in a daze. "Nina, why don't you just take the rest of the night off," he said without masking his annoyance.

She looked up at him with a glint in her eye. "Yes, Master."

He turned away from her before he could bite out another word and waited where he was until Gerald was inside the foyer.

"Hello, Gerald!" Stephen took a deep breath to calm his nerves and came the rest of the way down the stairs with his hand out.

"Stephen, my boy," said the old man, shaking his hand.

Stephen led the way into the living room and poured them each a finger of Chivas Regal.

"I hear congratulations are in order," said Gerald.

"Oh yes?" said Stephen, almost choking on his drink.

"I've been talking to your father. Apparently, there is a new lady in your life?"

"Herman, yes." He smiled. "You met her the last time you were here."

"The little girl?" Gerald raised his eyebrows. "I had a feeling."

"Don't get your knickers in a knot, I haven't done anything inappropriate with her." Stephen gestured for Gerald to sit.

"Well, good for you," said Gerald. "I did always think you'd end up with Marcy though."

"Her name is Margaret. And no. She's a good friend. That's all."

"You've always had your pick of the girls. You're blessed with your father's good looks."

"Herman is different though. She's the one I'm going to spend the rest of my life with, if she'll have me."

"Well then, congratulations really are in order," said Gerald, lifting his drink high.

"Thank you." Stephen tipped his glass in return.

"And what about the servant girl? Will you get her pregnant right away?" Gerald watched Stephen hasten to the door to close it, without pausing in his questions. "Or will you wait until you're married like your father did?"

"She's pregnant," said Stephen in a low voice. He walked back to the sofa but he was too anxious to sit.

"But you haven't told your little girlfriend."

"No, I haven't. Not yet."

"Nor have you told your parents yet that they're going to have a grandchild."

"I only found out myself last night."

"You're worried about how your mother will react, I imagine."

"Considering how she took the news about Reed, I am."

"But this one won't be her husband's baby."

"No, it will be her own flesh and blood," said Stephen.

"You have a point." Gerald knocked back his drink. "You have some tough conversations ahead of you, young man. Are you happy about the child?"

"I am, actually. I want to raise it myself."

"Very noble of you," said Gerald, handing Stephen his glass for a refill.

"I don't really think it's nobility. I want to be a father the way mine was to me. I've always felt a little sorry for Reed, not knowing for so long who his real father was."

"What if your little Herman doesn't feel the same way? Will you let her go in favor of the baby?"

"Again, not what my father was prepared to do," Stephen said, shaking his head. "I suppose I'm hoping for a miracle." He finished his scotch and poured another round.

"I sincerely hope you get what you're looking for," said Gerald, taking his glass from Stephen. "The curse has taken a great toll on your family."

"With any luck, this will be the end of it."

There was a small knock on the door; Stephen crossed the room to open it. Herman and Margaret waited on the other side, elegantly dressed in formal black for dinner. Herman smiled when she saw Stephen's tie; it matched the stones in her bracelet perfectly.

"Come in," he said to the two ladies, though he could barely take his eyes off Herman. Margaret went directly over to Gerald as he rose arthritically from his seat.

"Marcy! Lovely to see you again." The elderly man took Margaret's hand and leaned forward to receive a kiss on the cheek.

"Nice to see you again too, Gene," she said smiling.

"Funny girl," he said, chuckling at her joke.

Gerald turned toward the door where Herman and Stephen were kissing. "Put her down, Stephen! Let the old man have a look at this beautiful girl you've become so fond of."

He walked over and took Herman's hand. "My, haven't you grown up in three weeks," he said, admiring her.

"I'm watching you, Gerald." Stephen grinned.

"Very protective, this boy." Gerald cocked his head in Stephen's direction. "He'll take good care of you."

"He has been," said Herman, smiling.

He hooked her arm in his and led her to the sofa. "Have you been enjoying yourself here on the estate?"

"Very much, yes."

"And I heard you have a performance to show us tonight after dinner?" He extended his hand for her to sit, and he took the seat beside her.

"Yes, Gerald," said Stephen in an attempt to rescue Herman from the old man's attentions. "We are doing our first public performance tomorrow at a child's birthday party."

"Children?" Gerald lifted his gaze to Stephen. "So, none of those naughty tricks you were doing overseas then?"

"No."

"Shame," said Gerald, turning to Herman again.

"I'm not sure Herman would be ready for anything that complicated on her first time out," said Margaret, to interrupt whatever Gerald was going to say next.

"Is that what they were? They didn't look that complicated to me."

"Did you go to Japan to see Stephen perform?" Herman asked. Stephen was happy that she seemed much more socially at ease than when she had arrived, as though she was starting to fit in to the life he hoped to shape for her.

"Yes. Very interesting country, Japan. Beautiful," Gerald was saying.

"I've heard," said Herman.

"And I love the language," Gerald continued. "Did you know Stephen is fluent in it?"

"No, I didn't know that."

"Why don't you say something to her in Japanese,

Stephen?"

Stephen smiled at him, "I'll say something to you in Japanese that I wouldn't say in English in front of a lady if you don't stop mauling my girlfriend."

"*Touché*," said Gerald. He leaned toward Herman and said, "That's not Japanese."

"I know," she said, laughing.

"Where's my drink?" Gerald asked.

"This must be it," said Margaret, reaching for the only abandoned glass in sight. "Do you need another?"

"You could top it up for me, my dear." Gerald smiled at her thankfully.

Margaret topped up Stephen's as well and poured one for herself.

"Herman?" she asked.

"Oh, no thank you. I'll just have some wine with dinner."

"Good girl," said Gerald. "Don't let these two influence you."

***

Hours later, satiated with roast beef and red wine, Stephen and Herman stopped outside her bedroom door. They said goodnight to Margaret and watched her continue up the spiral staircase, leaving them alone.

"Here we are again," said Herman.

"Here we are again," Stephen repeated.

"I'm nervous about tomorrow."

"Please don't be. We'll be great together. Just like we were at dinner tonight."

He stood close, their lips inches apart.

"I'm looking forward to being able to go that way," she said, pointing toward his room, "instead of this way," she cocked her thumb over her shoulder, "at this point of the evening."

"So am I," he whispered.

The electricity pulsing between them was palpable, like static. Each waited for the other to move first. At last, Herman broke the conductivity.

"Better get some sleep."

"Yes," said Stephen.

He leaned in for a kiss, keeping the rest of his body at a distance from her. He knew if he touched her anywhere but her lips they would remain locked together for a very long time. He said goodnight and left her there, breathless, both of them to go to bed alone.

CHAPTER 24

The next morning, Margaret joined Stephen at the dining room table. "What's Herman up to this morning? She passed me, rushing up the stairs."

"She just went up for a shower," said Stephen, picking up his coffee cup to drain it. "We have to get to Mark's early to set up before the kids arrive." He reached for a card that was nestled amongst a dozen red roses in a crystal vase on the table. "Mark sent these for you, with an invitation for us all to go out for dinner tonight."

She took the card, glanced at it, and tipped the cup beside her plate to see if there was anything in it yet. "Sounds like fun. Shall I come with you, or am I going in my own car?"

"That depends on whether or not you plan to come home tonight," Stephen said, propping his elbows on the table.

She raised her eyebrows. "What are you suggesting?"

He gave her a lopsided grin. "That after dinner you might get lucky."

"Do you think so?" She plucked an apple out of a bowl on the center of the table and took a bite. The juice ran out and dripped off her chin before she could catch it.

"If you keep that up, definitely," he said, making a conscious effort not to wipe his own chin.

"Then I guess I'm driving. We'll be going somewhere swanky?"

"Probably."

"So, I guess wearing a fig leaf is out?" she asked, waving the apple.

Stephen laughed.

"What?" she laughed with him. "I haven't been properly laid in ages."

"In that case, I'll have Hawkins clear lots of space for the hundreds of roses you're sure to receive."

***

Stephen and Herman left for the Standish residence at ten o'clock, a full two hours before the performance was scheduled to start, and one hour before the guests were to arrive. They were greeted at the door by a butler, who explained that Mark would be down to see them shortly. He was presently aiding his young daughter, Tracey, in the important task of choosing between two dresses.

They were led down a long, carpeted hallway and into the room they were to perform in. Several dartboards on one wall suggested it was normally a game room. Chairs sat in rows before a stage area set up by Stephen's hired hands, and a few spotlights waited to be plugged in. There wasn't much the magician and his assistant could do until the next load arrived; it included the costumes, makeup, and props.

"Are you still nervous?" Stephen asked her as they sat in two of the front row chairs.

She reached out and put her hand over his. "No, not as long as you're with me." She smiled at him and he smiled back. He was about to say he felt the same way, when he heard Mark's voice. A second later, the man appeared in the doorway.

"Stephen!" he said and walked over, hand already extended as they stood.

"Mark, how are you?" Stephen asked, shaking his hand.

Mark's classic blond-haired, blue-eyed good looks

were brought out by the pink button-down shirt he wore, likely in honor of the party.

"I'm doing great, how are you?"

"I'm fine, thanks. May I present my assistant, Herman?"

"Nice to meet you ... Herman, is it?" He shook her hand.

"Yeah, strange for a girl, I know," she said. "It's nice to meet you finally."

They talked about the logistics of where the party was taking place and how Stephen would make his entrance. Meanwhile, the props and the makeup arrived, but without the costumes. Stephen made a quick call to Margaret to ask her to bring them, and Herman excused herself to put on her makeup. Mark gave her directions to the nearest powder room.

"Pretty girlfriend you have there," said Mark after Herman had left.

"What makes you think she's my girlfriend? I introduced her as my assistant."

"Oh come on, it would take a blind person to miss the way you look at each other."

"Ha ha, okay. I'll give you that one."

"I'm guessing she doesn't know you knocked up your servant?"

Stephen raised his eyebrows and stared in muted surprise.

"Word gets around, man," said Mark, shrugging.

"That fast? What the fuck? I've only known a couple of days myself."

"You know how the servants talk. They've been back and forth between here and your place all day today and yesterday. What are you screwing the hired help for anyway, when you have Herman?"

"Call it a moment of weakness," said Stephen. "And

153

anyway, Herman's still underage."

"Aha, I see. You going to get the servant an abortion? Your girlfriend might never find out."

"You're kidding, right?"

"Yeah, fat chance."

"Nina won't abort the baby, and I'm not big on the idea either," said Stephen. "I love kids."

"This one's gonna cost you."

"I hope not too much," said Stephen, gazing in the direction Herman had gone. It was more than he wanted to contemplate. "So, dinner tonight?"

"Yes. I'm looking forward to spending some time with Margaret. She hasn't changed much since university. You and she aren't still …"

"No." Stephen shook his head, saving Mark from saying what he was about to. "We're just friends. That's all we've ever been."

"Really?" Mark seemed genuinely surprised. "That's not what I heard."

"Okay, let's just say our involvement has never been a romantic one." Stephen scratched his head. "What is it with this community and everybody talking about everybody else? Doesn't anyone have a life of their own to worry about?"

"Not when you're a celebrity, I guess," Mark said, slapping Stephen on the shoulder.

"A celebrity? Here in Kingston?"

"People have been talking about your homecoming for a while. Even before Margaret started promoting you. Posters from your overseas shows have been going up all over the place."

Stephen had a good idea who was responsible for that; Nina had been keeping herself busy.

***

The lights came up, and the little girls oohed and aahed when they saw Herman in her sparkling dress alongside Stephen in his top hat and tuxedo. He started off with a few simple tricks with flowers and colored scarves, and then he called Margaret and Mark up to be volunteers. He tied their four hands together and held a sheet up in front of them, pulling it down a second later to reveal them tied together by the feet instead of the hands. The children were absorbed when Stephen, perched on a stool, told the story of the beautiful Princess Tracey (whose name just happened to be the same as the birthday girl's), and they were beside themselves with delight when the bunnies made their appearance. After the final bow, Stephen put his arm around Herman and whispered in her ear, "You were brilliant."

They stepped to the edge of the stage area, and the girls rushed past them to pet the rabbits. Herman went back to ensure the animals weren't afraid, watching out the corner of her eye as the parents who had stayed behind surrounded Stephen. He glanced at her occasionally and smiled.

Being around the children gave Herman a pang of regret for having left Chad behind. She knew he'd have enjoyed the show too. His enthusiasm for magic had the makings for a life-long passion. She decided to call him, the first chance she had.

At four-thirty, Stephen and Herman got into the car with the promise to meet Margaret and Mark at a restaurant downtown at seven o'clock.

"I want to phone home," Herman said as they drove home. "But I don't want to talk to my dad."

"The house phone number is unlisted. You could hang up if he answers, and he'll never be the wiser."

"Good. I'll take my chances."

LINDA G. HILL

***

When they arrived at the house, they retired to Stephen's office and closed the door behind them. He plopped down on the sofa and watched her dial her parents' number in the dim light of the desk lamp, thinking that it would soon be time to take the old storm windows off the back of the house and open them up. Herman's expression changed from frown to smile when someone answered at the other end.

"Hey Chad! How are you doing?"

She asked if her mom was okay and whether Chad was taking good care of himself. When she inquired about her dad, she looked at Stephen.

"I don't know, maybe. I'll have to ask the man I'm staying with. Maybe when school finishes for the year." She listened for a moment longer and then said, "Take care of yourself, okay Chad? I love you. Bye."

She pushed the button to end the call and placed the phone on its charger.

"Did he ask you if he can come to visit?"

"You caught that, eh?" she said, moving to sit beside him.

"I wouldn't mind at all. But if you want him to come and live with us, you'll have to get your parents' permission. We can't just take your brother."

"I know," she said. "He's okay for the time being. My dad's back on the road. He arranged with Chad's friend's mom to take care of him. Chad's not usually at home. He just happened to be there. Apparently, my dad has someone coming in to visit my mom, too."

Stephen put his arm around her and squeezed her tight. "Are you comfortable with the situation for now?"

"As comfortable as I can be, I guess." She leaned against him and together they reclined on the sofa.

They were locked in a kiss when Stephen heard a light

knock at the door. He sat up straight before he called, "Come in."

Hawkins opened the door. "Sir, may I have a word with you in private?"

"Sure." He kissed Herman on the top of the head as he stood, saying he'd be right back. He joined the administrator on the landing. From the top of the stairs, Stephen glimpsed Aunt Aggie haunting the foyer in her raincoat, clutching her purse and eying him with a black stare.

"What is it?" Stephen asked, turning to Hawkins.

"It's Nina. She has been having stomach cramps, Sir. Lotta and I both thought you should know. She and her mother are at the hospital now."

Stephen felt a sudden heat travel through his body, as though the blood in his veins had risen a few degrees. He looked at his watch. They were expected at the restaurant in less than an hour.

"Which hospital is Nina in?"

"She is at Kingston General, Sir."

He calculated the amount of time it would take to get to the hospital and home again by car; he couldn't make it before he was due to go to dinner. There was only one way.

"I need a ride to the hospital. Get the car, and I'll be downstairs in two minutes."

"Yes Sir," Hawkins said.

Stephen stepped across the landing to the wardrobe, to retrieve a large tome—a leftover from his coven days—that contained spells. He looked up the one he needed and memorized the words. In a box of show supplies he found a length of rope. Leaving it by the door, he chose an outfit for Herman to wear for dinner and slipped through a hidden door directly to her room to place it on her bed. When he returned to his office, Herman was sitting in the same spot, waiting patiently.

"I'm sorry, I have to go out," he said, crouching before her.

"Why? Where do you need to go?"

"I can't explain, but I promise I'll be home before it's time to go for dinner. Go and get yourself ready. I put something on your bed for you to wear tonight. I hope you don't mind. It's an extremely sexy outfit no one has worn before."

"Okay …" Her worried look tore him apart. He kissed her lips hoping it would erase her expression, but it didn't.

"I love you," he said, touching her cheeks with both hands.

"I love you too," she said.

He smiled at her and stood. "I won't be long."

He heard her say, "Bye," before he closed the door behind him. He grabbed the rope and ran down the stairs.

On his way out the front door, he caught another glimpse of Aunt Aggie.

"If you hurt her, you dirty little prick, I'll crush you," she warned as she swung her purse at his head. He ducked even though he knew it wasn't real. Hawkins waited at the car regarding him, stoic and expressionless. Stephen slid in behind the wheel, and took off as fast as he dared go.

When they arrived at the hospital's emergency entrance, Stephen left the keys in the ignition and told Hawkins to take the car home. With the rope in hand, and the words in his head, he strode into the hospital. He found Nina in a cubicle, sitting propped up on a stretcher and sipping a cup of apple juice through a straw. Her mother sat on the edge of a chair at the end of the bed.

Nina smiled widely. "Master! You came!" Lotta stood and went to her daughter's side as Stephen pulled the curtains closed.

"How are you feeling?" he asked as he stepped over to the other side of the bed.

"Much better. Thank you, Master. The doctor said it was probably nothing, but I should sit with my feet up for a few days anyway, just in case."

"Take whatever time you need."

"Yes, Master."

"There's something I'd like to do." He held up the rope. "Lotta, I know you don't like the Pagan rituals I believe in, so if you want to leave for this ..."

"No, that's fine, Sir. I'll stay and watch." She crossed herself and grasped a handful of bed sheets, squeezing until her knuckles whitened.

He took the cup from Nina's hand and placed it on the table beside the bed. "Lie down on your back please," he said gently. "This won't hurt."

When she was in position, he handed her the rope. "Please tie a knot in this. Don't strain yourself tying it too tightly."

She did.

"Now, concentrate on speaking to our baby. Hold the knot in both hands, over your heart, and repeat after me." Stephen placed his hands on the rope with hers. He looked into her eyes as he spoke the spell.

" *'My child, may you grow strong in the warmth of my womb*

"And come safely into my arms

"To live a long and healthy life.'"

They remained unmoving for a few moments after the spell was spoken. Nina blinked and a single tear ran from the corner of her eye; Stephen brushed it away with a fingertip.

"I apologize for not saying thank you for this," he said, placing one hand on her tummy.

"Thank you, Nina. I will love this child all the days of my life."

"As will I, Master. As I love you, Master."

"Don't go there, Nina." He strained to keep the edge

out of his voice. "Just focus on staying well now, for the sake of our baby and yourself."

"We'll take good care of her, won't we, Nina?" Lotta looked from her daughter to Stephen. "That was a beautiful speech, Mr. Dagmar, thank you for coming all this way to say that to her."

"Thank you, Lotta. I care very much that this pregnancy goes to term and our baby is born healthy." To Nina, he said, "If you have any more serious pains, please lie quietly. Then when you're able, think of these words as you tie another knot in the rope. Keep it, and undo the knots when it's time to give birth. It will help ease our baby into the world."

"Thank you, Master. I will keep it safe."

Stephen turned and peered through the curtain to make sure no one was coming.

"I have to go," he said. "Please check that I haven't left anything behind. Lotta, please keep me updated on Nina's condition."

"I will, Sir," she said.

Stephen looked at his watch. He checked one more time outside the curtain, and satisfied that no one would notice, he closed his eyes and visualized all that he was wearing and everything on his person, and then he pictured his bed at home. From the women's perspective, he disappeared with a short whistling noise from where he stood, with nothing to prove he had been there but the rope he had left behind.

He awoke five minutes later, sat up on his bed and abruptly collapsed. Too soon. The time it took to wake up and recover enough to function depended on the distance traveled. Even transporting twenty feet could leave him dizzy enough to fall, unable to rise for a few seconds. It was rarely worth doing, and one of the reasons he didn't use the power of transport in his shows. Two minutes later he tried again. Finding himself still giddy but determined not to be late for dinner, he stood anyway. He staggered to the bathroom to splash water on his face but realized when he looked in the mirror that he was still wearing eyeliner and eye shadow from the show. There was no time to deal with that. Instead, he crossed to his wardrobe.

By the time he was changed, he felt completely himself. His outfit consisted of a pair of black pants in a soft cotton, with legs so wide that they appeared to be a full-length skirt when he stood still. He stood before the long mirror on his wardrobe door and tucked in his black, sleeveless, high-necked tank top. Over that, he wore a see-through silk, knee-length coat with cuffs and collar of velvet. The coat was black, with fine shimmering-red swirls throughout the fabric. He returned to the bathroom to brush his hair to a silken black shine that matched what he wore, then he stepped out the door at the same time Herman walked through hers, right across the hall.

"Oh, you're back! I didn't see you come home."

"I must have snuck in. You look fantastic." He smiled and held her at arm's length to get a better look.

"So do you," she said, admiring his unusual clothes. "I don't know how to tie a tie though." She held up the black necktie that came with the black satin man's-style suit he had given her to wear. Her trousers were tight on the thighs and flared at the calves, with a blazer that came just to her knees. A black shirt with diamond cuff links, the black tie, and platform heels finished it off. She wore her sapphire bracelet over top of her left cuff.

Stephen put the tie in place under her collar and stood behind her to do it up. "I like it when your hair is up." He breathed on the exposed back of her neck as he knotted the tie, making her squirm. "We're going to be the sexiest couple in the restaurant. I think we should go dancing afterward, what do you think?"

LINDA G. HILL

"Sounds great," she murmured.

He spun her around and kissed her. She was almost as tall as he in her heels.

"I like it when you choose my clothes," she said.

"That makes me happy." He kissed her again, arousal stirring within him. "We'd better go before I get too carried away."

Outside, Hawkins held the car door open for Herman. Once they started off, she asked the inevitable question.

"Are you going to tell me where you went tonight?"

He felt her eyes on him. "I'll tell you tomorrow. Tonight, let's go and have fun, okay?" Taking her hand, he glanced at her long enough to see that she was thinking what to say. He waited quietly for her response.

"As long as you don't decide to disappear again tonight," she said finally.

"I've disappeared enough for one day, don't worry."

"Okay then."

"Okay then," he repeated, squeezing her hand gently.

He set his mind to not thinking about Nina, or tomorrow's confession, for the rest of the night.

CHAPTER 25

The waterfront hotel restaurant was filled to capacity with well-dressed diners. The *maître d'* recognized Stephen at once. He led them to the table where Margaret and Mark were already seated with a bottle of champagne on ice. A floor-to-ceiling window provided a beautiful view of the setting sun over the water, and a candle flickered on the table, adding romance to an already rich atmosphere.

Mark, dressed in a suit and tie, stood and shook Stephen's hand. Margaret looked elegant in a red silk Oriental-style dress.

"You both look so gorgeous," Margaret exclaimed with a smile.

"Thank you." Herman smiled back, feeling giddy with happiness. "It was all Stephen's doing."

Stephen pulled out the chair beside the window, and Herman sat facing Margaret. He settled into the seat beside her and placed his arm on the back of her chair as Mark filled up their wine glasses.

While the three friends caught up on each other's news, Herman gazed around the room. She noticed a few people stealing glances at them and whispering—most of them were women.

"Ignore them," Margaret said to her confidentially across the table.

"Is it always like this?"

Margaret nodded.

She shrugged it off and said, "Stephen suggested we go out dancing after dinner."

"Oh, what a great idea," Margaret said, loud enough to interrupt the men's discussion. "Stephen thought it might be nice to go out dancing after dinner," she told Mark.

"Sounds like fun," he said, smiling at Margaret and then Stephen.

The waiter approached and poured water, and Stephen ordered another bottle of wine. The man took a second glance at Herman; she thought for a moment he would ask her for identification to prove she was old enough to drink, but when Stephen said a pointed "Thank you," he simply nodded and turned to go, as though he had just remembered who he was serving.

The conversation flowed, and Herman realized with a comforting bliss that she'd found what she had left home to search for. Stephen had become, in an astonishingly short time, her family.

After dinner, when talk turned to leaving the restaurant, Herman and Margaret got up to use the powder room.

"Three," Margaret said as they walked away from the table.

"Three what?" Herman asked.

"When we come out of the restroom, there will be three women at our table talking to Stephen. That's my prediction."

"I say four." Herman grinned at the idea of a game.

"Gentleman's bet?" Margaret raised her eyebrows.

"Sure."

Before they returned to the table, Herman opened her purse, intending to refresh her lipstick. Inside she found an extra lipstick and lip liner.

"Where did this come from?" she wondered out loud.

Margaret looked over. "Stephen must have slipped it

into your purse while you weren't looking."

Herman stared blankly.

"He keeps it in the car, for emergencies."

"Lipstick emergencies?"

"He likes to wear it when he goes out, and sometimes when he performs, depending on the show."

Herman lifted the lid to check the color.

"I can't imagine him in lipstick. Even ... what is this, gray?"

"You'll like it, trust me."

"Well," said Herman, dropping it back into her purse, "you haven't been wrong yet."

On the way back to the table, Margaret held up three fingers and Herman held up four.

"Wow, you're good," Margaret said when they caught sight of the table. A woman in a short skirt occupied Herman's chair, sitting sideways to face Stephen, and three others stood crowded around him. Herman couldn't see her boyfriend, but she could see Mark. He stood as they approached the table. The woman in the short skirt jumped up, gracing Herman with a look of apology mixed with resentment. Herman smiled at her. Stephen stood to welcome her back, and all four ladies scattered. He pulled her close and kissed her cheek.

"I missed you," he said. She smiled at him with self-satisfaction. When they were all reseated, he reached over and held her hand atop the table.

Mark put his arm around Margaret and said something to her to make her laugh. Herman was happy for the woman who had so quickly become her friend.

"Do we know where we're going then?" Stephen asked Mark.

"Yep, let's go, shall we?"

They followed Margaret and Mark in his car to what Stephen described as an exclusive club. When they pulled off the main road and into a short driveway, Herman squinted out the window, surprised at the architecture of the building.

"Is this a train station?" she asked.

"It used to be Kingston's Grand Trunk Railroad station. It burned down a few years ago. They restored it and turned it into a bar."

"I love it," she said.

"Yeah. Not as traditional as ours inside, but they've done a good job restoring the outside."

She caught the word "ours" when he referred to the station at home, and she felt the warmth of inclusion in his voice.

He pulled into a parking space and turned the car's interior light on.

"Can I get my lipstick and liner out of your purse, please? And if you have any eyeliner in there, I'll take that too."

"Why did you put it in here if you knew you'd be doing it in the car?" she asked, rooting through her bag.

"I wasn't sure. And besides, I wanted to give you a heads-up. If I just put it on, you might not have recognized me or something."

"*Riiight,*" she said, handing him the cosmetics.

He opened the visor mirror and put on some eyeliner first, and then applied the lipstick and liner to his lips so expertly that she thought he must have been doing it for years. After a few adjustments, he closed the mirror and turned to her. The transformation was astounding. Margaret was right, once again.

"You're beautiful," she sighed. All she wanted to do was kiss him.

"Not nearly as beautiful as you."

"I'm not sure I want to share you."

"I don't really want to share you with all the guys who

are going to be ogling you either. But we do need to get out of the house once in a while."

"The men looking at me aren't near as bold as the women that hang all over you," she said, sounding horribly jealous to herself.

"I'm not afraid of them. Neither should you be."

"Before we go, I wanted to ask you something." She took a deep breath, knowing what she was about to ask would sound distrustful, but she couldn't help it. "When we got to the restaurant in the hotel, the head waiter recognized you. Is that because you're famous, or ..." She stopped herself before she could utter the words, *Do you go to the hotel often?*

He smiled. "My family owns the hotel. The whole chain of them, actually. Worldwide. We'll be staying in them any time the tour hits a major city."

Her jaw dropped. "Okay then."

"It's nothing," he said with a wave of his hand. "It's my dad's business. Should we go dance?"

She stared at his perfect lips. He leaned across until his face was an inch from hers.

"Don't worry, it won't come off," he breathed. He kissed her quick and light, followed by another and another. With his hand on her right hip under her blazer, he pulled her toward him. She ached to be closer to him. She wished there wasn't a storage compartment and a gear shift between them.

"Let's continue this on the dance floor," he suggested, his breath ragged.

"Good idea." She sat back and took a deep breath while she waited for him to come around to open her door.

They met their friends at the entrance. Margaret looked as ruffled as Herman felt. "Hot in the car," she commented.

Margaret fanned herself. "You could say that. I think I need the powder room again."

From behind her, Herman caught Mark's mention of Stephen's lipstick; she listened, curious to hear Mark's opinion, and heard him say, "Great, now even I want to kiss you."

Stephen laughed.

The two couples entered. Loud and somewhat industrial music with a heavy, contagious rhythm and raspy vocals blasted into the dimly lit room from hidden speakers.

"I think I'll stay with Stephen for a while," Herman yelled to Margaret over the noise.

"Probably a good idea. Mark your territory. I'll come and find you. Ask Stephen to order me a glass of white wine."

Herman nodded. She held Stephen's hand as they weaved their way between tables and through the mass of sweaty bodies. Stephen was right. Not only were the women looking at him, the men were watching her, as well. Being noticed after so many years of essential invisibility was an odd sensation. It had happened when she went out with Margaret too. She thought she could live with it. With her head held high, she walked through the crowd physically attached to arguably the best-looking man in the room. *Life couldn't be better*, she thought as she smiled to herself.

They found a table against the wall farthest away from the dance floor and ordered their drinks. Stephen pulled out his phone. Herman leaned over and saw that he texted to Margaret, "Usual table." She showed up five minutes later, looking impeccable.

"Long line-up," she said to Herman. "Why aren't we dancing yet?" She took a sip of her wine, grabbed Mark by the hand, and led him to the dance floor. Stephen offered his hand to Herman and they followed behind. Despite the fast beat and the heat, they danced close together. Stephen moved as the music carried him, and Herman followed his lead, getting caught up in his rhythm. A saying that went, *dance like nobody is watching* crossed her mind, and she did exactly that. Soon, she and Stephen were kissing as though no one was watching. He opened her tie and left it hanging around her neck. Beneath her fingertips, she felt the strength of his arms, his muscles just visible beneath the thin material of his coat. He loosened the top three buttons of her shirt and ran his fingers from her collar to her armpits, and down her ribcage to her waist. Holding her there between his hands, she felt his arousal as they danced. She nuzzled against him in invitation, feeling ready, eighteen be damned. This, out on a public dance floor, was the closest she had ever come to sex, and it was exciting, it was forbidden, and it was perfection for being enwrapped in the love that she felt for him. and he for her. Herman felt his breath coming fast and his heartbeat pounding in both his chest and his throat where her lips gently kissed and licked. He lifted his hand from her waist up to cup the back of her head, and he turned his head to kiss her, just once.

"Do you have any idea how much I want you?" he growled, his eyes dark with a fiery reddish glow at the center. "Or how perfect you are to me, or how much I love you?"

Overwhelmed by his passion, she could hardly speak. "I think so."

"Saying the words … it's nothing. I want to show you." He put his lips to her ear and breathed, sending shivers from her head to her toes.

"I want that too."

He breathed deeply once again and whispered, "Soon."

The song ended, and to Herman's surprise, they had an audience made up of half the dance floor and the tables that bordered it. Stephen glanced around without self-consciousness, but mostly his eyes and his dazzling smile were on her.

They returned to the table and found Margaret and Mark holding hands, looking hot but happy. Margaret drained her glass and held it up for Stephen to see. He nodded. She motioned for Herman to follow her.

As soon as they were far enough away from the music that they could speak normally, Herman asked Margaret if she thought it was safe to leave the guys alone.

"We can't be watching them all the time," she replied. "We'll end up feeling like their mothers."

Herman laughed. "As long as he's not signing some girl's tit," she said. Yet while they waited in line for the restroom, concern built up inside her. Unable to push away the vision of Stephen surrounded by women, she forced herself to remain calm and take her time.

She still hadn't shaken the sensation as they headed back to the table. Then Margaret stopped suddenly and turned around.

"Why don't we go back," she said.

"Why?" asked Herman, feeling a rush of dread. She leaned around Margaret to see what her friend had. As though she had predicted it, a young blonde woman stood in front of Stephen with her top hiked up to her collar bone, both breasts bared. He sat smiling before her, a marker poised, intent on signing his name.

"That's it, I'm leaving." Herman headed for the door.

"No, no, no," said Margaret, grabbing her by the arm. "No you aren't. He owes you an explanation at least, don't you think?"

Herman turned back for one last look and saw Stephen glance up from his task. He dropped the pen on the table and made a beeline toward her through the crowd, leaving a wake of gawkers; Margaret's tight grasp on her arm was all that kept her there. She heard Margaret grumble at him that he'd better know what he was doing.

"What the hell *are* you doing?" Herman asked him,

both angry and confused.

"Nothing that matters." He shrugged, an infuriating look of unconcern on his face.

"It matters to me!"

"Give me your hand," he said, taking it anyway. He placed it on his fly just beneath his belt and held it there.

"What do you feel?"

She glared at him. "Nothing."

"Exactly." He released her hand. "And what do you feel when I hold you close?"

She didn't answer. Margaret walked away, apparently satisfied that Stephen did, indeed, know what he was doing.

"Herman, this is my life. It doesn't change. It won't change. As long as I go out in public, there will be women throwing themselves at me. But there is only one girl in this world who turns me on and that I love, and that's you."

She regarded him. "I don't see how you can be faithful to me with all that temptation."

"It's not even a temptation. You are the only one I want. Only you."

Herman thought about how women reacted to him: the hangers-on at the restaurant, the girl at the ranch where they'd picked up the stallions, the ladies in the foyer when she'd first arrived at the house, and she knew he was right. It was something she would have to get used to if she wanted to stay with him.

"Do you really need to touch them?"

"No. In fact I didn't touch her. Only with the pen.

"Please come back to the table with me. Please." He smiled in encouragement and lifted her hand to his lips and bowed. "Princess of my heart, love of my life ..." he looked at her from beneath his eyebrows, and she grinned despite herself.

"Fine," she said.

They returned to the table, and Herman sat beside

Margaret. The older woman patted her hand and said into her ear, "Brave girl." Stephen squeezed her other hand, and she turned to look at him.

"Dance?" he asked. She nodded.

A slow song began as the foursome stepped on to the dance floor. Stephen slid his hands around Herman's waist, and she crossed her wrists behind his neck and leaned back. The music washed over her and she swayed, trusting that he wouldn't let her fall. He rested her on his knee, cupping her head in his hand.

He bit her neck a little too hard. *Love hurts*, she thought and with that, decided to spend the rest of the evening in oblivion of anything but him.

He accompanied her the next time she went to the restroom, taking his lipstick to re-apply it in the men's room mirror. She came out to find him waiting with a lady at each side. It struck her that all the women who had approached him were beautiful—much more so than she considered herself—and she thought perhaps it was their own beauty that gave them the confidence to speak to him. His head was lowered and he smiled at something one of the women said directly into his ear. When he looked up and saw Herman, his face changed. His expression softened, though he still smiled.

"There's my love." He stepped away from the two women and took Herman into his arms. He kissed her deeply with those perfect painted lips, and through slightly slit eyes she could see that at least one of the girls was staring at them; at his lips kissing hers.

"Ready to go?" he asked her, their faces still close enough to touch.

"Yes," Herman replied, thrilled to her core.

He took her hand, and they walked away without looking back. It was as though he had forgotten the women existed.

***

Just before the bar closed, Margaret took Herman aside and asked her if she'd be all right with Stephen for the night if she went home with Mark. Herman said she would, her thoughts swimming with happiness. Being alone in a house with the man she loved made her feel grown up, even if they weren't going to sleep together.

Once outside, Stephen said he needed to have a quick word with Margaret. He left Herman with Mark.

"You and Stephen make a great couple," Mark said, sliding his hands into his jacket pockets as they strolled toward Stephen's car.

"So do you and Margaret."

He nodded. "I hope we will."

"You seem to be off to a good start."

"It's been a long time coming. I guess you know we met in university."

"I heard."

"Tracey was already three years old, and I was engaged to her mother. But I was pretty attracted to Margaret, even then."

"It just wasn't the right time, huh?"

"I believe everything happens for a reason. I think she and Stephen needed each other. They were never apart."

"You don't think they need each other as much now?" Herman turned to look at the two of them, heads bowed in conversation beside Mark's car on the other side of the parking lot.

"Maybe not now that Stephen has you. I've never seen him this ..." He stared off into the distance, looking for the right word. "This concentrated on a girlfriend before. If I know Stephen at all, I'd say he really cares about you."

Herman shivered a little inside as the smile spread across her face.

"I don't think anything will separate them completely, though," Mark continued. "Can I ask you something personal?"

"Sure," Herman said, wondering what he could possibly want to know.

"Do you ever feel jealous of her? In terms of their relationship, that is."

"No," she answered, without hesitation.

Mark exhaled audibly as though he had been holding his breath. "That's good to know. Thank you. Margaret said you're a good friend."

"She said that?"

"Does that surprise you?"

"It's just that I've never really had someone who considered me a friend before. At least not since I was little."

"You have one now." They reached Stephen's car, and he looked across the parking lot. Herman followed his gaze. Margaret gave Stephen a quick hug, and the two started back toward Herman and Mark, arm in arm, their heads still bowed. Stephen said something that made Margaret laugh.

When they reached Herman and Mark, Margaret went to her new beau's side and he put his arm around her.

"It's been fun," Margaret said, smiling. "You guys have a good night."

"Not as good as you will," Stephen said, grinning back.

"You'd better not," she said. "Behave yourselves!" She wagged a finger at them and turned with Mark to return to his car.

"We'll try," Herman replied. She kissed Stephen and looked into his eyes. "Will we?"

"We'll behave," he said.

"Spoil sport," she said and slapped him on the bum.

He laughed and opened the door for her to get in.

When they arrived home, Stephen unlocked the front door and stared at her for a moment. She thought he might pick her up and carry her over the threshold, but he simply leaned in for a kiss. Hand in hand, they went to the living room and he poured them each a glass of wine. He helped her off with her blazer, and they cuddled up on the sofa to watch the end of an old movie on television. By the time the film finished, Herman was yawning.

A few minutes later, in their customary place outside her bedroom door, he stood close enough for her to breathe in his natural, masculine scent. She was happy he didn't wear cologne the way her father used to, years ago.

"I want you to know how much I love you." His voice held an edge of desire in its depth. "I want you to know that as strange as it seems since I've only known you for under three weeks, I feel as though you are the one I will spend the rest of my life with." He shook his head. "I've never even been tempted to say that to anyone before."

She looked into his eyes and saw sincerity. "I always wondered how I would know when I was in love," she whispered. "Now I know, so I believe you. Because I feel the same way. I just … know. You are the one."

He began to kiss her gently, but she pulled away.

"I don't want to wait," she said. "If we both feel the same way about each other, why do we have to?" She swallowed hard. "I want you to make love to me, tonight."

He regarded her, searching her face as though a thousand ideas were racing through his head.

"Not yet," he said. "It's not perfect yet."

She thought about how she had felt earlier in the evening when he left unexpectedly, and she felt the same butterflies as she did then. "Maybe you're right," she said, staring at his collarbone.

He placed his hands on her cheeks and tipped her chin up so she would look at him as he spoke.

"When it is perfect, you will know and so will I. And then there will be nothing in the world that can come between us."

She wrapped her arms about his neck and he kissed her, not holding anything back. Every part of her body, every nerve, every fiber of her being felt his love where their bodies met, and with everything she had in her, she returned it.

He left her quickly, vanishing through the secret door in the wall opposite, leaving her with a wetness on her cheek that could only be a tear. It wasn't until she reached up to touch it that she realized it was her own.

CHAPTER 26

The birds sang their song of spring in the tree outside Herman's window, and the sun's rays beamed across her pillow, waking her up the next morning. She stretched, hopped out of bed, and threw on a pair of jeans and a t-shirt, determined not to miss breakfast with Stephen. When she didn't find him in his room, she ran down the stairs to the dining room. It was empty but for one of the kitchen staff, a middle-aged woman with loose blond curls, who told Herman that Mr. Dagmar had gone to the barn earlier and hadn't returned yet. Rather than wait, she decided to get a cup of coffee from the kitchen and head out to the barn to meet him. On such a beautiful day, it seemed a shame to miss the opportunity to go for a ride together.

As she passed through the kitchen door, she overheard Patsy, the pale, mousy girl who Herman knew was friends with Nina, talking to the new dish washer; a tall, socially awkward woman in her mid-twenties who had been trying to fit in for the past week. Seeing the gossipy inclination of Patsy's head, Herman stopped to listen. She said Mr. Dagmar had been at the hospital the night before, and that he'd cast some sort of spell on someone.

"Stephen was at the hospital last night?" Herman asked Patsy, making her jump.

He must have gone after they had retired for the night, because surely if that's where he'd gone before dinner, he wouldn't have kept it secret.

Nina walked in, and all three turned to her.

"Nina, do you know why Stephen was at the hospital last night?" Herman asked.

The young servant smiled like someone who had been given a long-awaited gift. "He was there to visit me."

"Why were you in hospital?"

"I had stomach cramps. I'm pregnant," Nina explained with a sparkle in her eye.

"But why? What does that have to do with Stephen?"

"Master came to bless the baby and myself, so that I wouldn't miscarry."

Herman was confused, or she desperately hoped she was.

"Maybe you should sit down, Miss Anderson. You don't look well," Nina said, sounding almost genuinely concerned.

"I don't want to sit down."

"Miss Anderson, I'm so sorry." Nina placed her hand on Herman's arm; she shrugged it off.

"For what?"

"It wasn't my intention to come between the two of you. I hope you believe that."

Herman stumbled out of the kitchen into the dining room, Nina right behind her.

"Why are you following me?"

"I only want to make sure you're okay. I'm so sorry," Nina repeated.

Herman turned on her. "You're sorry about what? Just tell me in plain English. What are you talking about?"

Nina, with an expression of surprise that she hadn't figured it out for herself, exclaimed, "Miss Anderson, my baby is Master Dagmar's baby as well."

"No, it can't be." Herman shook her head, trying to shake loose the incredible foolishness that had spewed from Nina's mouth. She looked down at the servant's belly. In her tight pants, it was completely flat. It made no sense.

"I'm sorry," Nina said once again.

Herman turned away. She headed for the front door in an effort to escape what she didn't want to believe, but Nina followed her. She bumped into Margaret on her way in.

"What's going on?" the older woman asked.

Herman turned and saw Lotta standing in the doorway to the dining room, wringing her hands.

"I'm afraid I have upset Miss Anderson," Nina said, bowing her head.

"Why?" Margaret asked Nina. Her eyes shifted to Herman, to the tears streaming down her cheeks as she looked up to her friend for support.

"A baby?" Herman choked the words up past the lump in her throat.

Margaret's gaze shot to the young servant. "Where's Stephen?"

More confusion washed over her, and she began to feel sick. "You knew?"

Margaret looked over Herman's head at Lotta. "Go and get Stephen," she ordered the woman. "*Now!*"

"I'm sorry, Miss Flowers," Nina was saying. "But Miss Anderson was going to find out sooner—"

"And you took it upon yourself to tell her?" Margaret snapped.

"She asked," Nina said. "And I told her as gently as I could."

Herman missed the rest of the conversation. She ran up the stairs to her room, rifled through her drawers to find her old belongings, and stuffed them into her backpack. When she turned to go, she saw her bracelet on the bedside table where she had left it the night before. She hesitated for a moment while she cuffed at the tears that blurred her vision. She didn't want anything Stephen had given her; she grabbed it and threw it across the room before she ran out.

On the landing at the top of the stairs, she paused. Margaret still stood before Nina in the foyer. The girl's hand was pressed against her cheek as though she'd been slapped.

Herman charged down the stairs before anyone could think of a reason to stop her. Then Stephen walked out of the dining room and she halted halfway down.

"What's going on?" he asked Margaret.

He followed Margaret's gaze up to Herman. Looking at him felt like a stab in the chest. She doubled over as she lifted her backpack onto her shoulder and hurried past them all to the door.

"Herman, wait," Stephen said, reaching out to her.

"Don't touch me!" she yelled without looking at him.

Margaret caught up with her in the doorway. "You have to let Stephen explain," she said.

"Explain what?" Herman spat. "I think it's pretty self-explanatory. How far along is she?" she asked, turning on Stephen.

"Two weeks," Nina answered. Stephen glared at her; his hand twitched as though he could have slapped her himself.

Herman's stomach heaved, and she ran out the door to throw up in the flower bed.

"Come back in, Herman," Margaret said from behind her, after she had composed herself a little.

"Why? It's all been a lie." Herman wiped her mouth with the back of her hand and looked up at the woman she'd considered a friend until a moment ago. "Everything he's said to me has been lie. Even you ... Even you?" She winced. "What kind of sick ... disgusting ... who *are* you people?"

"We are exactly who you know we are. It's the situation that's not what it seems. Please, just let us explain. Then you can go if you still want to."

"I can go now. What the hell do I have to keep me here?"

"I need you," said Stephen, appearing in the doorway.

"Too fucking bad!" she screamed as loud as she could. "Find someone else who fits into your friggin' dresses!"

Herman stomped down the steps to the driveway, hauling her backpack onto her back, the image of Nina's smug face hovering sickeningly in her mind. Stephen chased her and grabbed her arm, pulling her around to face him.

"I meant everything I said last night," he said, looking her in the eyes. "I love you."

"How can you say that?" Herman's voice sounded unnaturally high to her ears. "You don't even care about me enough not to have sex with her." Her last four words were choked off by the tightening in her throat; she turned away, stepping out of his hold on her arm so he wouldn't see the new flood of tears that blinded her.

"Herman, I had no choice."

Her anger returned as she rounded on him. "What do you mean you had no choice? You couldn't do it with me so you had to screw *somebody*? Are you going to tell me you had sex with Margaret next?"

Margaret, standing behind him, shook her head, an expression of utter despair clouding her features in the bright sunlight. "It's not like that, Herman."

"Please let me tell you the whole story," Stephen said. "Let me help you understand."

Margaret came down the steps to where they stood and held out her hand. "Please," she said.

"I'm not going back in there." Herman glanced at the front door, expecting to see Nina. She wasn't there.

"Anything you want," said Stephen.

Herman dropped her backpack and rubbed her eyes clear of tears that refused to cease. Beside her, Aunt Aggie demanded that she listen to the prick and that if she didn't, she'd regret it. She doubled over and forced the water from her eyes with the heels of her hands and clenched her teeth, holding in a scream.

"Talk then!" She couldn't look at him. She stared at the ground and listened through the ringing of emotion in her ears.

"My family and the Currys have a curse on them that goes back three generations."

At that, Herman looked up and stared at him with her mouth open. There were so many things to say in response to what she'd heard, that she was unable to form a coherent sentence.

"A curse," she finally blurted out. "You're telling me a curse made you want to have sex with your servant?"

"I didn't want to. I had no choice." His pain darkened his eyes.

"And a *curse* made you do it."

It was Margaret who answered. "You've seen the powers he has. Is the idea of a curse so unbelievable?"

"Exactly," Herman said to Stephen. "You have powers. Couldn't you have just reversed this so-called 'curse' and saved us all the trouble?"

"Lotta's grandfather tried to fight against it and failed. In the process, his daughter died in a fire with my father's sister. I have a sister. It's too much to risk that it wasn't a coincidence."

Herman squeezed her eyes shut.

"I know it sounds like a bad excuse," Stephen said as the specter of Aunt Aggie chanted in her ear, "*Stand your ground and listen to the prick.*"

"Fine!" she screamed to drown out the noise. "Tell me about this curse then." She pressed her hands to her temples in an attempt to squeeze the annoying voice of the ghost out of her head.

"My great-great-grandfather had an affair with the housekeeper, who was a Curry. His wife who was a Dagmar by birth, discovered them together and put a curse on both families."

"And the curse states what, that you have to keep repeating history?"

"Something like that. The curse was worded that the Currys had to sacrifice freedom and stay in servitude of the Dagmars, and the Dagmars had to sacrifice faithfulness to the one they loved the most, until there is no possibility of Curry blood that is not mixed with Dagmar blood. Nina is the last of the purebred Currys."

"And Reed ..."

"Is my father's son," Stephen finished for her.

"Well that explains the sick relationship you have with your servants. How did your mother handle Reed's existence?"

"My father didn't tell her until Reed was sixteen years old and had to come and work here. When she found out, she went ballistic. She couldn't stand to live under the same roof as Lotta, so she decided to leave. My dad left with her. Because he loves her."

"And now that it's your turn, you've been waiting for me to come along so you'd have someone to be unfaithful to?"

"That's an awful way to put it."

"But it's true." Herman glared at him with a black look that would have withered anyone weaker. "I showed up and that gave you the perfect excuse to start having sex with her. How long have you been doing it? Since I arrived?"

"Herman, don't ask me that. I only did it for as long as I had to, in order to get her pregnant. I never have to touch her again. I won't, ever, touch her again."

"And now you expect me to stay here? Your mother

didn't, why should I? Will Nina and her family be able to leave now?"

"Not yet. Not until she can't have any more children."

"Then I will," Herman said. She picked up her backpack and started down the walkway.

"After the baby is born," Margaret called to her. "She's agreed to have a hysterectomy. Then they can leave."

"And what about until then, Margaret? What am I supposed to do? Live with his *lover*? Live with a man who *says* he loves me and then turns around and has sex with someone else because he *had* to?" She turned on Stephen. "You did it for as long as you *had* to? You expect to be pardoned because there's a curse, so you could tell me you love *me* and not touch *me*, but then you could go and screw Nina? Get your rocks off that way and not even feel guilty about it because you *had* to do it?" She turned to walk away again.

"*No,* Herman." He grabbed her arm to stop her. "I felt like hell every time. It was never about the sex. I swear to you, I didn't touch her any more than I absolutely had to, and I still feel as guilty as hell. I've never disrespected anyone as much as I did her."

"Except for me, you mean."

"What else could I do?" he asked, his voice pleading. "I fell in love with you. I couldn't help that, any more than you could."

"But you could have helped having sex with another woman. Did you consider that?"

"Of course I did. But to do that would be to pass on the curse to any other children I have with you. Rather than do that, I chose to make the sacrifice myself."

"And you made it my sacrifice as well. You sacrificed our relationship."

"Please don't say that. I'm sorry, Herman."

She tried to put herself in his position and couldn't do

it. All she could feel was the pain of his betrayal, taste the sickness of it in her mouth.

"I'm sorry too," she said and walked away from him. He didn't try to stop her.

She made it halfway down the driveway before she collapsed on the pavement. The gravel bit into the skin on her knees through her jeans but she didn't care. It felt good. No physical pain could compare with the pain deep within her ribcage that Stephen had caused by loving her and then ending her world so completely. She put her head down on the asphalt in front of her knees and cried like she had never cried before. After a few moments, she felt a hand on her back.

"How?" Herman asked, once she realized it was Margaret kneeling beside her. "How can he tell me that he wants—" Her breath hitched in her throat and she took a moment to breathe. "That he wants to spend the rest of his life with me and be lying to me the whole time? How did he make me believe him?"

"Because he was telling you the truth, Herman," Margaret leaned down to speak close to her ear. "He does love you, with all of his heart. The sick thing about it all is that it was necessary for him to love you in order to end the curse."

Herman tried to wrap her mind around the idea, but it kept going in circles.

"Why couldn't it have been someone else he fell in love with? Why me?"

"Because you *are* the love of his life, and he is yours. You believe that, don't you?"

More circles.

"I did yesterday."

"If you really believed it yesterday, then you'll believe it tomorrow."

"*The slut is right Herman,*" Aunt Aggie said in her ear.

"Go away!" Herman yelled at her.

Margaret started to get up but Herman placed a hand on her leg to stop her.

"I wasn't talking to you," she said to Margaret.

"I'm not going anywhere until you go back to the prick. You know you want to, you snot-nosed little brat."

"I have to go," Herman said to both Margaret and the ghost.

"At least let me drive you somewhere," Margaret offered.

"No, I need to be alone. Aunt Aggie is with me, don't worry about me."

"Do you have any money?"

Herman nodded and dragged herself onto her feet. She started down the driveway again without looking back. Blood trickled down her leg but she didn't care. She had to get as far away from the real pain as she could.

CHAPTER 27

ow? How could he do it? How? How could he do it? It was the question Herman marched to. The rhythm was her anger, her confusion; it was what kept her momentum. She pushed the memories of the happy weeks leading up to this morning out of her head the second they appeared. She thought if she let them in, she might sit on a rock on the side of the road and never get up.

How? How could he do it? She watched the gravel, the pavement, the sidewalk, all without seeing them. When she did finally look up, she was on the outskirts of the city. She knew where she was going. Back to the train station. Back to where the best part of her entire life had begun. She couldn't hold it in any longer. She sat on a slate of rock in the ditch and let the tears come. The little things, like never again having the opportunity to ride double on a horse with Stephen or see the look in his eyes when he said he loved her, overwhelmed her with grief. She mourned the loss of their plans to go camping on the island and perform shows together, the missed rehearsals and the chance to experience his magic. And her birthday—tomorrow was going to be the best day ever. Aunt Aggie patted her shoulder the way she had when Herman was a little girl and employed every swear word Herman had ever heard to describe him.

She exhausted her crying and began to walk again, talking to the ghost as she trudged along under the thin warmth of the sun, unable to understand why it still shone.

"He's a slimy little creature who can't keep his dick in his

pants, but you've got to give it to the prick. At least he didn't sleep with you."

"Now I know why."

"He gave you his heart and his soul but not his filthy body."

"Do you really think so?"

"I'm not telling you anything you don't already know."

Herman was well into the city when she stopped at a gas station with a restroom and a store. She had had more than enough time to miss being at the house, but she didn't see any way around having to deal with Nina, even if she could find it in her heart to forgive Stephen, which she wasn't sure she could do.

"How can you forgive the prick for fucking around on you?"

Herman stood at the sink in the gas station's restroom. She narrowed her eyes at the ghost of her great-aunt behind her in the mirror.

"I can start by understanding that he really had no choice. But did he? Couldn't Nina have had a hysterectomy in the first place?"

"Would you if you were in love with him and that far beneath him? Wouldn't you do whatever you could to get him to fuck you?"

"So, she wouldn't do it?"

"What do you think?"

"But he did still have sex with her while he was telling me he wanted me. And that he loved me."

"Animals mate all the time. Does love have anything to do with it?"

"He's not an animal."

"Isn't he? Aren't all humans just animals?"

"Okay, what about the baby? Will he want to be part of its life?"

"You'll have to ask the prick that."

"Don't you know?"

"Even if I do, I can't interfere."

"Aren't you interfering now?"

"I'm not telling you anything you're not already thinking."

"Do you even exist?"

"The prick saw me without knowing I existed."

"Will you please stop calling him 'the prick'!"

"Not since I saw it." Aunt Aggie smiled and disappeared from her line of sight in the mirror. When Herman turned, the ghost was sitting on the toilet, doubled over with laughter.

"Why are you laughing?"

"Because you're defending him."

Herman left the restroom and wandered back into the store to return the key and buy a can of Coke. She carried her drink outside and sat on a curbstone beneath a newly budding maple, and considered what to do next.

She thought about what Stephen had said about his father: he must have had sex with Lotta while he was married. Reed was younger than Stephen by about a few years. Therefore, Stephen's father had a secret affair and somehow kept it from his wife, even though the affair produced a child. Stephen had chosen to get it over and done with before there was any physical betrayal. He had left her virginity intact. She could walk away with no more than the emotional scars he had bestowed. Unless staying with him could heal those as well.

Could she forgive him? What about the baby?

You'll never know if you don't go back.

Herman wasn't sure if it was Aunt Aggie or herself who said it.

She finished her Coke and returned to the gas station to ask for a phone book. There were no Dagmars in the directory. It took her a moment to remember Mark's last name. Standish. She recognized the street name and called the number of the house she had visited just yesterday: it seemed like a lifetime ago.

Mark picked up on the second ring.

"Mark? Hi, it's Herman. Can you tell me what Stephen's phone number is?"

"I can do you one better. He's standing here beside me."

Herman froze. She expected to have more time to think before she spoke to him. In a panic, she hung up.

***

Herman walked, focusing on the patterns the runoff water made on the pavement to keep her mind away from what she would have been doing at home with Stephen. When she looked up, a restaurant named "Sakura" stood before her. She remembered Stephen mentioning the word as the name of a flower he loved, that they celebrated with festivals in Japan in springtime, and she wondered if it was some kind of sign.

She had directions to the train station and though her first thought was to leave town, she considered the alternatives. If she decided to stay one night in a motel, she would deplete a third of the money she had left home with. She was determined not to return to Ottawa, to her mother. A lot of difficult decision-making and planning had gone into leaving the first time — she didn't know if she'd have the guts to do it again. If she took the train to Toronto, there was more chance of finding a youth hostel, which wouldn't cost her as much as a motel. But she wasn't sure she had the heart to go that far away from ... *from Stephen*. His betrayal hurt her. It made her sick. But whenever she remembered the way he made her feel when they were happy, she realized she didn't think she could live without him. If he was sincere about his feelings toward Nina — and in fact all that she'd observed was a coldness that agreed with everything he had told her today — then perhaps she could trust that he would be faithful to her from now on, in every sense of the word. She wanted to believe he would. Then she thought about what he'd done, and anger boiled up inside her and made her want to scream.

She reached the crest of a hill and spied the pointed tower of the Kingston train station. Seeing it brought back the memory of her arrival—of the nerve it took for her to get off the train with the tall, dark, handsome man who had become her life—and the tears welled up suddenly, as she choked on a sob. She knew she had to talk to him one more time, if only to say goodbye.

Rather than continue to the train station, she turned left at a set of lights and stopped at an inexpensive-looking motel just up the street. She wrote her name and her old address and phone number on the little form she was given, knowing Stephen would be able to find her if he really wanted to. She wondered if he would.

She was about to walk away from the counter with her key, when the clerk, a nice-looking Indian man with a kind smile, called her back.

"Someone called about an hour ago and left his number for you." He handed Herman a note. On it was written, "Stephen." She got as far as the "613" exchange before her eyes blurred over with tears.

"Thank you," she said and turned away to look for her room.

She chucked her backpack on the floor beside the window that overlooked the parking lot and sat on the bed. Attempting to take her mind off Stephen, she turned on the old box-style television. She flicked through the channels until she came across the same movie they had cuddled up to watch, much earlier that morning. Herman turned off the TV, curled up in a ball on her side, and cried herself to sleep.

When she woke up, the light had dimmed and dusk was settling. The empty room reminded her of where she had been at the same time the day before, sitting in a restaurant, laughing and talking with her friends and the man she loved, and she felt a new inrush of pain and emptiness. A flood of tears lasted for as long as she could stand the physical pain of hunger.

Slapping herself into some semblance of respectability, she left with a ten-dollar bill and her key, and headed toward the Tim Horton's down the street. She brought a bagel and a coffee back to the room and ate in silence, concentrating on the mechanics of chewing and swallowing in order not to think about anything else. When she finished, she crumpled up the wrapper and looked over to the bedside table at the note with Stephen's name and phone number written on it. She knew deep down that only she herself could answer most of the questions she still had. The biggest of them all was whether or not she could live with his betrayal. And possibly with his child.

She dialed "9" according to the instructions on a grubby, worn-out sticker on the phone, and then the number on the note. He picked up after two rings.

"Herman?" He sounded panicked.

"Yes." It came out not much louder than a whisper.

"Are you okay?"

"Not really, no." A question dawned on her that she hadn't planned to ask.

"How did you know where I would go? You left your number here."

"I didn't. I left my number at every lodging in Kingston, hoping you hadn't left the city."

Herman smiled, despite herself. Maybe he did care about her, after all.

"I love you Herman," he said quietly. "I want you to come home."

Herman's breath hitched, but she managed to hold back a sob. The tears started to flow again. She took a deep breath before she tried to speak. "I need to ask you something."

He paused before he answered. "What do you want to know?"

"Were you going to tell me yourself?"

"Yes, I was going to tell you this morning. I was just waiting for Margaret to come over. For moral support. For both of us."

She thought about his answer and decided she was content with it.

"Why did you hesitate before you asked me what I wanted to know?" She needed to know she could trust him, and that pause had her more worried.

"Because some things will be harder for me to talk about. But I promise to be completely honest with you."

"Thank you," she said. "I suppose you know where I am now."

"Yes."

"Don't come." She shut her eyes tight, squeezing out a tear. A knot had formed below her ribcage. It felt like a stone. Like her heart had hardened and dropped. "I promise I won't leave Kingston before I talk to you again."

"Okay."

"I have to hang up now."

"Please remember what I said last night," he said. "I meant every word."

"So did I. Goodnight, Stephen."

"Goodnight, Herman."

She hung up the phone and tried to remember exactly how he had worded what he said. It wasn't until she woke up the next morning that it all clicked.

***

Before Herman lay down for the night, she perched herself on the bed and in the nicotine-colored light of the lamp, dialed Mark's house again, hoping Margaret would be there. Mark answered and asked her to wait; a moment later the woman she hoped was her friend came on and asked her how she was doing.

"I'm okay, I guess. I felt like you'd be a better person to talk to than Stephen about some things. I'm too emotional when I talk to him." She reached across the table for a box of tissues and held onto it, just in case.

"That's understandable." Margaret's voice was calm and soothing, and would stay that way throughout the conversation. "What do you want to talk about?"

Herman sighed deeply and braced herself for what she needed to ask in order to move forward.

"Is there really a difference between sex and making love?"

"Definitely."

"How do you know? How can you tell?"

"Sex is a purely physical act. Making love is so much more than that."

"But, you cared about Stephen when you had sex with him."

"Yes, I did. But that was a different thing again to what he did with Nina."

"What was it like for you when you 'just had sex' then?"

"We did it to fulfill a physical urge; at the time, we were both available and unattached. It's like going to a movie with a friend. It's different than being on a date, isn't it?"

Herman contemplated Margaret's words. She hadn't been on a date with a boy, as such, but she knew what it felt like to love Stephen and to want to go everywhere with him as a couple. Still, she needed to understand how he might have felt having sex for the sake of making a baby, if that's all there really was to it.

"So what did Stephen do with Nina?" She grimaced at her own question.

"There was no urge involved, nor was there any caring; it was purely to reproduce. He had to force himself to perform. He described it to me as torturous, almost like self-inflicted rape."

Herman sneered. "I wonder how Nina would describe it."

"She would probably say it was wonderful and romantic. She's happy with any attention Stephen gives her."

"And you believe Stephen's version of the story?"

"Of course I do, Herman. Has Stephen ever given you any reason to doubt it? Have you ever seen a knowing look between them? Have his actions toward you, or that you've seen toward Nina, ever disagreed with what he has told you?"

"No."

"Have Nina's?"

"Yes."

"Then whose version do you believe?"

Herman sighed again. "I suppose I'm trying to protect myself."

"I don't blame you, sweetie. Your heart is a precious thing to lose. But you know what, Herman? True love is a very rare thing. And that feeling you have that you were truly meant for each other is once in a lifetime. When it comes from deep inside, and you know without any doubt that you are supposed to spend your life with someone ... it's not something that everyone experiences. There are people who never know what you and Stephen have. Don't throw it away unless you're sure you can't live with what he was forced to do."

"You're sure he had no choice?"

"He asked me to watch. He was desperate to make sure

that when the time came for you to find out, he wouldn't be the only one whose word you'd have to take."

"That's sick."

"It was humiliating for all of us.

"Herman, he handled this in the way he thought best. He could have done it the same way his father did before him, but he didn't want to put anyone in the same position his mother faced. He saw firsthand what it did to her. Stephen and I have talked about this for years, and he decided a long time ago that he would rather sacrifice his only chance at real love than pass the curse on to his children. When you came along, it was as though his life was beginning and ending right before his eyes. He knew damned well that you probably wouldn't stay and put up with it. Who could? But at the same time, he trusted that the love you have for one another could withstand it. He also took a risk by not making love to you."

"How ... how was that a risk?"

"Had he made love to you, you would have been more divided, more hurt, but more likely to want to stay, even if your gut had told you not to. He'd have had more of a chance to keep you. He wanted to give you all the choice he could to leave if you wanted to."

"But, how would making love to me have made me want to stay more? Wouldn't it have just made me more angry?"

"Yes and no. You'd have been angrier, but on the other hand your love for each other would have been fully realized."

"So I would know what I was really giving up."

"Exactly. Now you can only imagine. And if you do realize it after you lose your virginity to someone else, it'll be too late. Even if you did return to Stephen, it wouldn't be the same. Wonderful maybe, but not the same."

"Not perfect." The words echoed with a familiar ring in

Herman's ears. She pulled a few tissues out of the box and clutched them tightly. "Thank you for talking to me tonight. I have a lot to think about."

"I know."

"It's all so confusing." She pressed the tissues to the bridge of her nose as the tears started to flow again.

"Oh, sweetie," Margaret said, her voice full of empathy. "I think you need to sleep on it. It's been a long day."

"Yeah, you're probably right."

"And if you need more time, just let me know. I'll pay for you to stay put as long as you'd like. Call me any time you want to talk, okay?"

"Thanks." Herman sniffed. "Goodnight."

She placed the phone back on the cradle and lay down beneath the dingy light of the lamp to shed another river of tears.

CHAPTER 28

*S*he arrives at the party, a living room full of people smiling and talking to one another, and she feels as though she has lived there before. She knows the smiling faces, but she can't remember any of the names, and she knows it's summer outside, and she knows that he will be here soon, so she stands in the corner and waits, trying not to be noticed.

Then he arrives. He says hello to people, but he looks at her standing in the corner and even as he speaks to others, he keeps his eyes on her. When he gets to her he smiles and takes her hands in his, and she can feel the warmth of his smile, and he asks her how she is, and she says she has been waiting for him.

"It's okay now," he says, dropping to his knees. "I'm here."

They are in a marketplace, holding hands. People are dancing, and they join in the dance. It is sunny, and the dance is joyful. Everyone is clapping and smiling, and she closes her eyes. She thinks to herself that it is strange to close your eyes in a dream, and she opens them again, and he is still there, only now they are alone. It is dark and they are in a room with a streetlight shining through the window, and they are lying on a bed, just as they were in the last dream. She dreams the dream in the dream she had before, and she knows she is dreaming it, and she wonders if it will go better this time; this time she isn't afraid. He holds her tightly to him and he says, "I'm here, and I won't leave you, ever," and she kisses him, and he returns her kiss, and she feels his love, his all-consuming, all-encompassing love surrounding her like his arms, and he says the word that he said before: "Perfect. You are perfect for me and we are the perfect fit for one another," and she wants to say something to him, but she wakes up …

Even before Herman opened her eyes, Stephen's words came back to her from their last night together.

"When it is perfect, you will know and so will I. And then there will be nothing in the world that can come between us."

The dream, she thought. She knew why she had held back, why he held back, and what had come between them. The dream that had scared her so badly was dispelled. The unknown was known. There was nothing left to fear. There was only love.

She opened her eyes to the same weak ray of electric light shining through the window that she had fallen asleep to. The numbers on the clock beside the bed glowed 4:32. She turned on the light and let her eyes adjust before dialing Stephen's number.

She heard a shuffling at the other end and a groggy, "Hello?"

"Stephen, it's Herman. I need to see you."

"Are you okay?" he asked, suddenly alert.

"I'm fine. I'm okay, just come, please."

"What's your room number?"

"Twelve."

"I'm on my way," he said and hung up.

As she put the phone down, a wave of nerves like a chill took over her body. She tried to lay back down and cover herself; that lasted a few seconds. Estimating that it would only take Stephen ten minutes to cover the three or four hours she had walked the day before, she stood stiffly and headed for the shower. Under the stream of hot water, she washed her body and her hair. Her shivering had ceased by the time she got out.

She slipped into the cheap, almost threadbare robe provided by the motel. Wrapping her long hair into a towel on top of her head, she set herself to wait. Her muscles clenched from her throat to her pelvis when she heard a soft knock at the door. This would be the test. Would she feel pain or happiness when she laid eyes on Stephen? She opened the door.

Seeing his face filled with worry and hope felt like finding someone in a crowd who she'd longed to see. Relief and joy flooded her as he breathed her name. He hesitated only long enough to read her expression and then with one step through the door, he reached for her like a man starving. She moved into the enclosure of his arms and let him devour her lips; need electrified every nerve in her body. He lifted her feet off the floor and kicked the door closed behind him, and then he pulled away to ask her what she wanted. Desire darkened his expression, but she knew it was entirely up to her.

"Do you love me?" She searched his eyes for the truth.

"Oh Herman, I love you with all my heart and soul," he whispered.

She kissed him as he carried her the short distance to the bed. He sat, Herman on his lap, straddling him.

"What do you want?" he asked again, his voice deep and gentle. His eyes, black with the hint of red that glowed in the dim light of the bedside lamp; his straight nose with the small bump below the bridge that was more pronounced in profile; his perfect lips, flushed with desire and shaped in a way any woman would kill for; his skin, darkened with a slight stubble; and his hair, messed from sleep and shiny, black as the night were all as she remembered seeing them before. Yet there was something different. There was a calmness to his need, as though he had fought through a battle and was now waiting to discover the outcome.

"I want you," Herman said with a deep exhalation.

"Are you sure?"

She saw him as she had felt him in her dream: in the first, with the hopeless sense of despair when he had left her, and in the second, with the profound sense of eternal, all-consuming love, and she knew that yes, she was sure. "I don't know what our future will be, but I know I have to be with you, or I won't have a future. I can't go back. Take me with you."

"Everywhere," he breathed. He drew her to his lips and kissed her, easing the towel from her head. His fingers ran gently through the wet strands, lifting her hair from her face and her neck as he bent to kiss her there, covering her in goose bumps. Shivering, she slid her hands up under his t-shirt and he yanked it off, watching her eyes. She gazed back, wanting to look at his body but afraid to at the same time.

"Look at me," he said as though he'd read her mind. Taking a breath, her gaze dropped to his chest, muscular and lean, his arms, strong and well-defined, and then to his hands as he undid his belt and pulled it through the loops. He stood, lifting her with him and turned around, placing her on the bed, on her knees, so they were eye to eye. He kissed her once and took half a step back. Her nerves flew skyward when his hands lowered to his fly, but her focus didn't waver. He must have seen her shiver; he put his hand out to take hers and lifted her palm to his mouth and kissed her there. She looked him in the eye.

"I won't hurt you," he promised. He stepped forward again and pressed his mouth against hers. She felt his hands move at his fly, and he stepped out of his jeans. Tentatively, she touched his back. She lowered her hands to his hips— they were bare. Then she looked down. What she saw there was much larger than she expected, but then, she had never seen a full-grown male in the nude before. Not in the flesh.

"Can I touch it?"

He nodded.

At first she was surprised at how hard it was, and then at how soft and silky was the skin stretched over it. But what amazed her the most was the pulse that beat inside it, in her hand; it was like she held the pinnacle of his energy. A moan from his lips brought her attention back to his face. With his eyes closed and his chin tilted up, his hands were bent like claws at his sides.

"I'm sorry!" she said, letting go, wondering if she was doing it wrong.

He opened his eyes and they were dark, but she wasn't afraid. "No." He smiled. "Don't be sorry."

His smile eased her nerves. She wrapped her arms around him and pulled him to her, feeling the hardness of him, the tenseness of him through the single layer of material of her robe. So close, she thought, to both of them being naked, being together. There was no doubt in her mind that she was ready.

Stephen kissed her mouth, her cheek, her neck, his hands were everywhere: her shoulders, her back, her hips, her legs. He lifted the hem of her robe and ran his fingernails lightly up the bare skin of her legs; up the back, he let it go, up the sides, he let it go, up the front … Her hands shot to the tie on her robe and she tugged at the knot until it came undone. She slipped it off her shoulders and knelt there, naked and surprisingly unashamed as he ravished her with his hands and his mouth. The roughness of his chin scratched deliciously the underside of her breasts as he took one and then the other nipple into his mouth. She opened her legs as his fingernails once again made the journey slowly up her thighs, this time between them. Before he reached their center, his hands scraped outward, around her hips, and he grasped her cheeks of her bottom as he stood straight, pressed himself against her pelvis and kissed her mouth all at the same time. Overwhelmed with desire, she leaned back, pulling him with her down on to the bed.

He held himself above her in such a way that the only places they touched were her nipples against his chest and the tip of his penis against her belly. He kissed her just below the ear, and she wrapped her legs around him, struggling for contact.

"Wait," he said. "I want to make sure you're ready."

"I'm ready," she gasped.

He smiled at her, and produced, out of thin air, a shiny square package.

Oh, she thought. The reality of what her body was urging her to do seized her. She hesitated only for a second.

"Take me. Do whatever you have to do."

"Do you trust me?"

She realized there was more to that question than just now, than just him making love to her. The rest of her life was in his hands.

"Yes."

He began again at her throat, kissing and swirling his tongue, and her shivers came back and with her goose bumps, her nipples tightened. She watched him lower his face and tease them one at a time with the tip of his nose, and then he laid his tongue flat against one, then the other and licked, and at the top of her thigh, suddenly, his fingers stroked upward. He stopped just short again, and she strained downward, urging him to touch her where no man had before. She looked down at him and met his eyes. He smiled as he moved down the bed, farther, until she could feel his breath on her sex. Still, he didn't touch her, but now she was suspended between longing and shame.

"You are so very beautiful, Herman," he said, though his eyes hadn't left hers. Without averting his gaze, he touched her. One fingertip. Her entire body tensed and her thighs jerked and closed around his ears, and then it was his tongue touching her the same way she sometimes touched herself in the dead of night. Her back arched, the back of her head pressing against the mattress, her heels digging into his back, she was aware only of his hands on her hips and the sensation of his wet mouth between her legs, and his tongue inside her, probing and licking and taking and giving. When she could take no more, she breathed, "Please, Stephen!" in a moan of excruciating need.

He parted her legs with his hands and slid up until his body covered hers. The face above her, framed by his black hair, was the one she had fallen in love with. And though there was a glint of deeper red in his eyes, his gentle, desirous smile reassured her.

"Herman," he whispered as the tip of his cock came in contact with her opening. "My beautiful, sweet Herman." He entered her, just a little, and it was a sensation like no other. The pulse she had felt in her hand throbbed and filled her with an energy that vibrated and consumed every nerve in her body.

"Oh my God," he moaned, his neck arching. He pulled out almost all the way and pushed himself in again and this time, finding no resistance, buried his cock inside her and paused. He lowered his head to look her in the eye. "Do you feel it?" he asked, his voice strained. "This is home."

She nodded and as her muscles clenched from her chest to her knees, she writhed with the pure fulfillment of his weight on her and his sex inside her. He began to move then, each time pulling out farther and thrusting harder: hard enough for her to feel pain but not so much that it was overwhelming. She felt the pressure of his need slowly rise as his thrusts become faster, and her own breathing was stilted and heavy as he moved deep inside, inching as he did toward climax. Her body seized in orgasm when she felt him grow, when he held his breath, when he cried out with his own release.

She waited for the grip of his orgasm to let him go and then he let out a short laugh of relief and he kissed her fully, deeply and passionately.

"I love you," he breathed between kisses. "I love you."

Under the weight of his body, she held him close and kissed him back, wishing she could stay this way forever. With Stephen inside her, with Stephen's love all around her, protecting her, keeping her safe and warm. She wanted nothing else from life but this.

"Don't ever leave me," she sobbed between kisses.

"I will never leave you," he answered.

She knew with all her heart that he never would.

CHAPTER 29

The morning sun rose on Herman's eighteenth birthday, lightening the room with its pale glow. She rested in the crook of Stephen's shoulder, relishing the warmth of his skin against hers and wished the sun would stay down, even as she looked forward to whatever the coming day had in store for her and her lover.

"Let's do it again," she mumbled into the musky fragrance of his shoulder.

He chuckled softly. "We've used up all the condoms."

"Can't we just not bother?"

"No, we can't. And besides, your stomach is growling. Shall I go out and get us coffee and something to eat? I can get some more condoms ..."

She squeezed him close and gently bit his nipple. "I don't want to let you out of my sight. If we really have to eat, let's go together. I've never gone out for coffee with you."

"It's definitely a day for firsts," he said, lifting her chin and kissing her deeply.

"Should we shower before we go out in public?"

He laughed. "We're going to look as though we spent two hours making love, why not smell like we have, too?"

"Do you really think people can tell just by looking at us?"

"Oh yeah."

"I don't care." She shrugged. "There are worse things than looking like you've been making love to the most beautiful man in the world."

She rolled over on top of him and grazed the rough skin of his cheek with her teeth. Being naked together felt so sinfully luxurious.

He gently rolled her back over. "We need more condoms," he said, his voice filled with lust.

"Where do you get all that self-control from?" she asked breathlessly.

"I have no idea." He gave her a peck on the cheek and slipped out of bed. Herman admired his rear aspect until he turned the corner into the bathroom.

She fell back on the pillow and looked up at the ceiling, enveloped in a sense of utter awe.

CHAPTER 30

They sat in a booth by the window at Tim Horton's, sipping coffee from paper cups with dark brown plastic lids and gazing into each other's eyes.

"Would you like to do anything special for your birthday?" Stephen asked with a smile.

"Other than make love to you all day? Nah. That's special enough for me." She fidgeted, not wanting to kill the mood but knowing there was no choice. "But first I think we need to talk about some other stuff."

The smile faded slowly from his face. "Anything, my love."

"What would you have done if I hadn't decided to come back?" Herman asked, thinking it best to start with a subject she was less emotional about.

"Other than be miserable for the rest of my life?"

"Other than that, yeah. What would you have done about the show?"

"Found a substandard assistant I suppose. The show must go on, as they say."

"Why substandard? I can't be that good; I have no idea what I'm doing."

"It's not about *what* you do." He reached out for her hand and squeezed it. "It's about the energy between us. I didn't fully understand it until this morning."

"I think I know what you mean," she said, remembering the electrifying pulse she felt the first time she touched him.

"I'm not sure how to put this delicately …"

"Because you've had other assistants who shared the same energy with you?"

"There's that, but …" With his elbow on the table, he rested his chin in his hand and gazed into her eyes. He remained in that position for so long, she thought he'd forgotten what he was going to say. Finally, he spoke again. "You are incredibly different from any woman I've ever met. It makes me wonder even more if you have a gift of your own."

She put her elbow on the table and mirrored his pose. "Explain."

He opened his mouth to speak and stopped himself again. At length, he took a deep breath and said, "You are the first woman I haven't been able to seduce with a look. By all accounts, you should have been begging me for sex when we met on the train."

Herman sat back and removed her hand from his, unable to think what to say to that particular revelation.

"It's not that I wanted to seduce every woman I looked at. In fact, it can get downright inconvenient. I've had to train myself not to look most women, and ten percent of all guys, directly in the eye."

"Is that why you love me? Because I'm a challenge?"

He smiled. "It's part of what attracts me to you, but no. I'm connected to you by this unique energy we share. I've never felt anything like it before. And the only thing I can surmise is that maybe you have something in you like I do. Something magical."

She relaxed again and took his hand. "I'm happy you feel it too. But I don't see why that would stop you from finding another assistant."

He shook his head. "I knew instinctively from the moment I met you that you would be my last. And luckily, I'll never have to look for a substandard assistant because

I'm never going to let you go."

She took sip of coffee while she psyched herself up for the next inevitable question.

"I need to know what you want to do about the baby."

"I want it to know who its father is, and I want to get joint if not full custody." He stared out the window for a moment. "I don't want to do what my father did with Reed. Both Reed and this child will inherit part of the Dagmar fortune, eventually." He turned to her. "I want all of my children, including the ones I hope you and I have, to know right from the start where they came from and what they stand to gain. It's only fair. But I doubt Nina will give the baby up and give me full custody."

Herman expected hearing Nina's name spoken out loud to feel like a knife to her gut but it didn't. In light of the past few hours, Nina was a concept. A poison she hoped could be washed away before it could possibly be re-consumed. "What about her? She'll have to stay and work at the house until the baby is born, I guess?"

"She only works two days a week."

"I'll only have to put up with her gloating two out of every seven days, then." Herman dropped her gaze to her lap, knowing she sounded bitter. She couldn't help it. She might never get over the fact that someone else was having his baby. But there was nothing that could be done about it. All she could do for the moment was not let it ruin what they had shared.

"Look into my eyes, Herman." He leaned across the table and she did too. "I will do everything in my power to keep her from antagonizing you. I'm not going to say I'll always succeed, but I know this pregnancy is a process that you and I will get through together. And once it's over and she is sterilized as she promised she would be, we won't have to deal with her directly anymore."

"So you won't have any contact with the mother of

your child?"

"Do you think I should?"

"No," she snapped, feeling her answer was purely selfish. She thought about the distance between her own parents and how much it hurt. Her ill will toward Stephen's unborn child felt uncomfortable. Unfair. Instead, she lashed out at the cause.

"Why was Nina ever even born? Reed would have been the end of the curse if she hadn't, wouldn't he?"

"That was one of my first questions when my dad told me about the curse." His upper lip lifted in disgust and he stared out, not at the beige building across the street, but into the past. "I was only thirteen years old, and I had to keep the secret from my mother that my father had been unfaithful to her. I knew Reed was my half-brother, years before he came home." Stephen shook his head. "It took a long time for me to forgive my father."

He sat silently, as if remembering for a moment, before he returned to Herman's question. "Nina was a surprise pregnancy. Lotta didn't plan to have her—not after the sacrifice she made in her own marriage. But Lotta is Catholic; she wouldn't have an abortion, so here we are."

Herman crossed her arms and sat back, her thoughts returning to Nina's pregnancy. "Do you expect me to help you raise it?"

"I don't expect anything of you with regards to the baby. But if you want to help me, I'll be happy."

"Forgive me if it takes a while to get used to the idea. I don't know what I'll think until it's separate from … its mother."

He reached across and held both her hands in his.

"No matter what happens, you need to remember that you are the only woman in my life who I love, and nothing will ever change that."

"I know that. I do."

"But …?"

"But don't be surprised if I freak out occasionally." She looked down at the table and then up into his eyes. "This morning with you changed a lot of things for me. I feel like I've changed. I don't know how I'm going to react to anything anymore. But do I have to find out right away?"

"No. We can stay at the motel another night. Or we could go to a hotel. It's up to you."

"I like our room," she said with a smile. "But as for going home … It's not that I don't want to go back. I do. In a way, I can't wait to get on with the rest of our life together. I'm just not sure I'm ready to face any of the Currys."

"Well then, why don't we just go to the closest drug store and then concentrate on each other for the next twenty-four hours?"

"Sounds wonderful." Her smile was strained with emotion.

"It will be."

They walked out hand in hand.

On the way back to the motel, Herman glanced back in the direction of the train station. A mournful whistle sounded as if in acknowledgment that it was still there, waiting, should she change her mind. She had left home a girl. Now she was a woman with choices. As she gazed into Stephen's smiling eyes, she knew she'd made the right one.

CHAPTER 31

Not a word had been spoken of the curse while Stephen and Herman remained in the sanctuary of the motel room. Instead, he had explored with her the wonder of their energy together. What he had said to her was true; he'd never been with anyone like Herman. So deep, so harmonic was their connection, that making love was like being inside the bubble of a dream: sometimes frantic and euphoric, always intimate and precious.

Now, in the warm dark-gray interior of the car, with what promised to be an early summer breezing through the windows, they drove silently home. Free to discuss the ramifications of Stephen's inevitable betrayal, neither knew what to say, nor where to start. His guilt put a pall on what should be the celebration of going home with the new lady of the manor. He longed for communication, for contact. He reached across to hold Herman's hand and she forced a smile. The comfort of her touch brought him momentary peace.

Whatever contentment he found on the drive home turned to unease as he braked at the front steps of the house. He saw Hawkins standing stiffly at attention in the shadow of the building waiting to greet them, and an irrational worry crossed his mind; what if the man had bad news about Nina and the baby? As his heart thumped in his chest, he forced himself to move slowly while Hawkins opened the passenger door and Herman got out.

She looked up at Stephen and he did his best not to

show his concern. She needed his support as much as he suddenly needed to get word of Nina, but he couldn't ask Hawkins about his daughter in front of her. Instead, he told Herman he had to check on the kitchen for dinner, feeling ashamed at his white lie. Herman's birthday celebration arrangements did have to be made, though not right away.

Hawkins carried Herman's backpack to the door and waited there. She glanced up at the man and back to Stephen. "Where should I unpack my things?" Her voice was hesitant and her tone, shy.

"Dinner can wait." He forced a smile and took her hand. Without lifting his gaze from her eyes, he said, "Hawkins, would you take Miss Anderson's things to the master bedroom?"

"Certainly, Sir." The administrator proceeded into the house and left them beside the car, locked in a kiss.

It was several hours before Stephen managed to get away. He repeated his excuse about arranging dinner and sent Herman off to talk to Reed about getting the horses ready for a ride out to the station. As he approached the kitchen door, he heard the unmistakable tone of gossip.

"… she had to be dragged out of Mr. Dagmar's room, kicking and screaming," said Patsy, the young kitchen maid who was Nina's friend. Some friend, he thought.

"No!" It was a voice he didn't recognize: the new girl, he supposed.

"I think she's delirious, personally. She was wailing about Mr. Dagmar driving his car into Lake Ontario and killing himself, and that it was all her fault."

"Wow. Is it true she's having his baby?"

Stephen chose that moment to open the door. The two girls turned back to their work, both struggling to simultaneously look busy and stare at him.

"Where's Lotta?" he asked Patsy. He wondered if the bright-eyed young woman, currently up to her elbows in dishwater, was the same gossip who had spread the rumor of Nina's pregnancy to Mark's staff before the party.

"She's in the dining room I think, Sir." It was barely more than a whisper. She batted her eyelashes at him, probably without realizing she was doing it.

Just then, the woman in question scuttled in from the dining room with a tray full of silver for polishing, and Stephen turned to her.

"Lotta, I need to speak to you in private."

He led his housekeeper across the foyer to the office and closed the door behind them.

"How is Nina?"

"She's locked herself in her room, Sir. She promised me she would come out to eat, but she said she won't come out for anything else until she has seen yourself, Sir."

"But she's taking care of herself?"

"Actually, I'm worried, Sir. I've noticed some of the alcohol in our house has gone missing. It's not a lot, mind you, but Reed and Hawkins deny having drunk it, and I know I haven't touched it, so unfortunately it seems Nina is the only one left."

Stephen sighed heavily. "I'd like you to get rid of whatever alcohol you have left in your home until I can speak to her myself. You can keep it locked up here in the house. Just get it out of arm's reach of Nina. Would you mind?"

"Not at all, Sir."

"Tell her that I expect her to work on Saturday as usual, as long as she is feeling physically well. I'll speak to her then."

"I will convey the message, Mr. Dagmar, thank you."

"I'd like you to have Hawkins make arrangements for caterers to come out to the island on Sunday. I'll be having a small party for Herman out there."

"Yes, Sir."

"I'll let you know the details when I have them."

He left for the barn, distracted with worry for the baby, even as he made plans to talk to Hawkins about changing the kitchen staff.

CHAPTER 32

As the Sunday morning sun rose on Herman's fifth day as lady of the manor, she slipped from beneath the covers and settled in a chair facing the bed. *Our bed,* she thought. She covered herself with the duvet they had thrown off during the night. In the light that peeked through the delicate lace sheers at the window, she watched Stephen sleep peacefully and listened to the birds twitter and twerp in the tall maple just outside. A thrill passed through her and she smiled to herself. She had never been so happy. She had begun to get used to the idea that she could act with confidence, despite the whispers from the staff that she was sure were about her. How she had been betrayed and whether or not she would last. Being ensconced night after night in Stephen's chambers was conducive to the dream. But it wasn't a dream. Still, she pinched herself often.

As she gazed at his face, resting in repose, she thought about his magic the night before. It was their first real performance in front of a large audience, and she'd been beside herself with fear. He had decided against doing the ladder trick, knowing how nervous she was. Yet once they took to the stage, she found that Stephen's stage-presence alone was enough to keep her smiling through the show. His confidence bolstered her own. She had felt uplifted on the stage with him, and not only because he had levitated her. Together, there was nothing they couldn't do. She knew it in her bones. Now, sitting in their bedroom, awash in the warmth of being in the presence of her lover, she thought that when the time came to perform with the ladder, she'd even be able to handle that with ease.

After the show, on an adrenaline high, they had had mind-blowing sex in the back of the truck, standing up in the box he used to make her disappear. Then a stroll, hand in hand, along Kingston's waterfront trail was followed by a romantic dinner, dancing, and home to spend the rest of the night curled around each other in their king-sized bed.

Today was a new day, and there was a surprise up Stephen's sleeve in celebration of her birthday. All he had given away was that it was to start with breakfast in bed. Sure enough, at eight o'clock on the dot, Lotta knocked at the door with breakfast for two. As odd as it felt to have Lotta in their bedroom with the pair of them partially clothed, Herman was grateful that there still hadn't been any sign of the housekeeper's daughter; Nina had been scheduled to work yesterday, but she hadn't shown up. Herman did her best to put the girl out of her mind. Nothing was going to ruin her day, least of all Nina.

Hours later, when the sun was high in the sky, they rode on horseback to the shore. A rowboat decked with garlands of flowers awaited them. Stephen took the helm and rowed them slowly out to the island in style, while she shaded herself with a frilly umbrella. The sun blazed brilliantly and the breeze softly blew across the surface of the chilly water, and never in a million years could Herman have imagined a more magical way to celebrate her birthday. Nor could she have imagined being so much in love with a man whose beauty, generosity, kindness, and intelligence exceeded that of anyone she had ever known; nor did she think she would ever want for more than just this.

As they approached the island, she saw balloons and streamers decorating the high deck of a house where three figures stood waving to them. She waved back to Margaret, Mark, and Gerald, happy to discover there would be a party just for her. Her last had been more than half her lifetime ago.

They reached the dock, and Stephen pulled the boat up close and held it steady for Herman to climb out. She waited for him to tie the boat up, then she wrapped her arms around his neck and kissed him.

"Thank you," she said, smiling.

"You're welcome, my love. Let's go party." He squeezed her tight and they walked hand in hand up a winding cobblestone path to the house.

Stephen led her up a staircase on the side of the building. They stopped at a landing halfway up and entered the house; outside, another flight of stairs continued directly to the deck. They climbed a spiral staircase much like the one to the playroom; at the top was a large living room with glass walls on three sides. The house was positioned on the point of the island, so every window provided a view of the water. The room reminded Herman of a comfortable, inviting ski lodge she'd seen on the glossy pages of a magazine. Overstuffed sofas that looked like they could swallow a person whole, and heavy, rustic tables made of lacquered logs filled the space. On the inside wall was a wide, gray fieldstone fireplace with a hallway on both sides. The one on the left, Herman assumed, led to the bedrooms; through the other she could hear people talking.

"Who else is here?" she asked.

"Caterers."

"Will we be spending the night here, too?" She glanced down the left-hand hallway.

"Yep. Margaret brought some clothes for you."

"You think of everything."

"I hope I haven't missed anything."

"Just this," she said, standing on her toes to kiss him.

"Now you're perfect." She smiled. "Until next time I require one of those."

"I shall try to anticipate your every need from now on," he said.

"'Atta boy." She pinched his bum and laughing, they went out through a set of sliding glass doors and onto the deck, to say hello to their friends.

She made her way around the glass-topped deck table, accepting happy birthday wishes as they each stood and gave her a hug and a kiss on the cheek.

"Has Stephen been treating you to lots of special birthday things?" Margaret asked her.

"It's been a wonderful day." Herman beamed, glancing at Stephen. He smiled back, affection shining in his eyes.

"Looks like our Stephen has been treating himself every bit as much," Gerald said, and Herman blushed.

Stephen, attuned to her embarrassment, took her hand to kiss it. "I'm a lucky man, Gerald," he said, locking her to his gaze.

"Yes, you are," Gerald agreed. "I haven't seen a couple so in love since your parents."

Herman smiled tentatively, not knowing if Gerald was aware of the curse and what it had almost done to Stephen's parents' marriage. "I'll take that as a good sign," Stephen said with a nod, leaving her none the wiser.

Their deck chairs, shaded by umbrellas and set in a semi-circle, faced the water to the west. To their right was the boat launch and the mainland, and to the south, the open water of Lake Ontario. Herman shaded her eyes and peered to the left. Below the level of the deck was another house: smaller, but of a design almost identical to the one they had come through. The smaller one had a deck that wrapped around only two sides.

Herman turned to Margaret and asked, "Is the other house for guests?"

THE MAGICIAN'S CURSE

"Usually the servants stay there. The summer kitchen is there, too. That house is air-conditioned. This one isn't."

"How does anyone sleep in this one in the summer?" Herman asked. "It must be hot."

"It has bigger windows and a nice through-breeze. And if it gets too hot, there are beds around the outside at the back of the house, on a screened-in deck."

Herman had a flashback of her nightmare, of a bed on a cottage porch. She shivered and pushed it from her mind.

As the sun traveled from south to west, they drank a lot and they ate a lot, they talked a lot and they laughed a lot. Mark, who was a riot once he got going, had Herman laughing so hard that she almost peed herself. After a spectacular sunset of ruby, coral, and amber on a backdrop of sapphire dusk, citronella candles and lanterns were lit by the dozen. Herman's birthday cake was served by staff she didn't recognize, and presents were brought out.

From Margaret, she received lingerie. To no one's surprise, Gerald jokingly suggested she model it right away. From Mark, she received a riding crop for riding the horses and potentially keeping Stephen in line, and from Gerald, she received a beautiful burgundy silk scarf, again, for potentially keeping Stephen in line, Gerald told her with a gleam in his eye.

Herman was surprised to see that there was also a present—a small, square box with a bow on top—from Stephen.

"But, you already gave me my present." She held up her left wrist with her sapphire bracelet; she had dug it out from behind a dresser on the floor of the guest room when they came home together.

"I couldn't resist giving you something else."

She lifted the lid off the box and found a ring wrapped in a small square of red silk. She plucked it out and turned it. A red stone, set deep in a wide band that was black as the

221

night, glowed in the candlelight as though a fire burned inside of it, reminding her of the mahogany gleam in Stephen's eyes.

"It was handed down to me by my grandmother," he told her. "She told me that when I met the love of my life I should give it to her, to keep her safe."

"What is it made of?"

"It's onyx with a garnet. Both are stones that represent protection."

Margaret leaned toward Herman to look at it. "It's beautiful," she whispered.

Herman tried it on the first finger on her left hand and it fit perfectly.

"It is," Herman agreed. "Thank you."

She stood to kiss everyone on the cheek. When she took her seat again, Stephen reached for her hand. She turned to look at him; for a moment, she couldn't figure out what she was seeing. His face was blurry, as though she was looking at him through a dirty window. An odd, queasy feeling hit her when she realized she was looking through the back of Aunt Aggie's head, as the ghost bent to stare into his eyes. Then her Aunt's words froze the sickening sensation in her gut.

"It doesn't protect her against everything, prick."

"Why, what's wrong?" Herman asked her great-aunt.

The three who couldn't see Aunt Aggie looked at Herman, confused.

"It's Aggie," Stephen explained to Margaret.

"I'll tell you later," Margaret mumbled to Mark and Gerald.

"What's wrong, Herman?" Margaret asked.

"I don't know, she's gone."

Suddenly the island below them lit up. Spotlights on the ground shone brightly on both houses.

"Can Aunt Aggie do that?" Margaret asked Herman.

Herman shook her head.

Stephen crossed to the south railing in two strides and peered over the side. Herman assumed that's where the light switch was located. She, and the rest of them, stood to join him. They all looked up when they heard Nina's voice from the deck of the smaller house. She was nude.

"She has to know, Master!"

"Oh my God," Margaret said.

Stephen took off along the deck to the stairs at a run.

"You need to know that we conceived our child here on the island," Nina called to Herman.

"You don't need to listen to this," Margaret said, taking her arm to lead her away, but Herman wanted to hear. She lifted one finger to stop Margaret from speaking.

"We lived here together for two days. My Master made love to me all over the island. He kept me naked, like this, for two whole days. He put his penis inside me and took me whenever he felt like it, and I accepted him every time with pleasure. The day we left here Master took me from my father's side and claimed me as a woman. He brought me up to his house one last time where we were wed before all of nature, where we created the child that rests now in my womb."

"Holy shit," Mark mumbled. Gerald turned away.

"He made love to me every day since you arrived, sometimes five times a day. Even after we conceived our baby, he—"

Stephen finally reached her and muffled her mouth with his hand, pulling her by the waist with his other arm along the deck and into the house.

Herman shook her head to clear it.

"Don't pay any attention to what she said. She's gone completely mad," Margaret said.

"No, it's okay. Stephen told me there were things that would be difficult to talk about. He wanted to tell me, but I didn't want to know."

She started for the stairs. Margaret reached out and took her wrist. "You're not going back for more."

Herman turned to her. "I'm not going to leave her alone with him. You said it yourself — she's crazy. Stephen might have a lot of explaining to do, but I'll do whatever I have to, to defend him against her in the meantime."

They ran down the stairs and up to the other house.

***

When Stephen reached Nina, all he could think about was shutting her up. He had missed half of what she said, but he did catch that in her opinion they had "made love." How many other fantasies she'd blurted out in the time it took him to get to her, he could only guess.

Whatever she might have said ceased to matter when he caught a whiff of alcohol on her breath. Rage heated his face as he dragged her into the house and deposited her on the sofa. He threw a blanket at her — the same one she had covered herself with the night he discovered she was pregnant. "What the fuck are you doing drinking? Do you *want* to lose the baby?"

"No, Master," she whimpered, wrapping herself in the blanket. "I love our baby, just as you do. I promise I won't drink anymore."

He swallowed the urge to touch her, to feel the baby's existence the way he had before. "Nina ..." He closed his eyes and exhaled some of his anger. "You *have* to take care of yourself."

He tensed again at the gentle squeak of the door opening below and footsteps charging up the stairs.

"But Master, that girl you're with has to know what you mean to me and what she is destroying!" Nina stood and dropped the blanket. She reached out for him at the same time Herman reached the landing.

"Don't touch him," Herman yelled.

224

Stephen fought another urge, this time to cover Nina with his body. To protect her.

Nina stopped short of physically connecting with him and turned to Herman. "Did you hear what I told you? You can't possibly want to stay with my Master after that."

"I heard everything you said, and none of it matters. I feel sorry for you, but it changes nothing."

"*You* feel sorry for *me*? I'm carrying Master's baby, and you feel sorry for *me*? My Master came inside me and we made a baby, and —"

"Nina! That's enough!" Stephen snatched up the blanket to wrap it around her again, but she turned quickly in the arc his arms made. She stood on her toes and attempted to kiss his mouth.

In three steps Herman was across the room, pulling the girl away from him by the hair. "I don't care if you're pregnant or not, I won't hesitate to hurt you."

"*Herman*," Stephen barked, and Herman let go of her and stepped back, wide-eyed. Nina dropped to the floor and he turned his focus on her, bending to take her face in his hands, to be sure she was okay. This time, it took all his might to resist the need to feel inside her, to check that the baby was alive. He had just enough sense in him to wonder what the hell he was thinking.

"Master." She looked up at him through tear-filled eyes. "Please, tell me you care about me enough to leave her and look after me and our baby."

Margaret appeared at Nina's side. "I've got her," she said as she covered the servant with the blanket.

Stephen's tunnel vision lifted, and he eased himself away from the sobbing girl. "Herman isn't going anywhere, Nina. You're being intolerable."

Reasonably satisfied that Margaret would take care of her, he stepped outside. He paced the deck, listening to Margaret on her cell phone ask Hawkins to come to the island to retrieve his daughter.

By the time he heard the door downstairs close, he was much calmer. He joined Herman where she sat on the sofa, her arms crossed, hugging herself. He sat and put his arm around her. She didn't respond to his touch.

"I didn't hear everything she said."

Herman snorted. "Why don't you tell me your version of the story, then, and we'll talk about the discrepancies afterward."

"Herman, look at me." He knelt on the floor to face her and took both of her hands in his.

"I know what you're going to say. You love me, and I'm the only woman you'll ever love, and you never felt anything for her. But what the hell, Stephen? Your mother didn't stick around for it, and I'd be willing to bet Lotta never got up to shit like this."

"She didn't. But we'll be out on the road soon."

"*Pfft.* I can't wait."

He looked down at his hands. "I'm sorry, Herman. I hate putting you through this. And I do love you, and you *are* the only woman I'll ever love. But that's not what I was going to say."

She waited while he chose his words.

"I wanted to say thank you for sticking up for me and for believing in me." He searched her eyes for the understanding he didn't feel he had the right to expect.

"How can I not? You've done everything in your power to prove to me you love me. Apart from your little episode here when you practically fell to your knees to make sure she was all right, I haven't seen an ounce of anything you give me, directed toward Nina. I know you must care about her; you have to."

She pulled her hands away and sighed. "I'll try to be okay with whatever you need to give of yourself to keep her sane. But it might kill me to watch."

Stephen thought about his urge to touch Nina in what would have been perceived as intimate and he shuddered.

"Just promise me that once the baby's born we can get rid of her," Herman continued, "and I'll promise to try not to kill her in the meantime."

Stephen felt the blood rise to his face again, and Herman sat back. "What was that?"

"What?"

"Your eyes. They went all red for a second. They did it before, too."

"I have no idea. Nothing like it has ever happened before." He wondered if there was more to his magical inheritance than the abilities he was already aware of. A call to his parents would have to be made soon; he made a mental note to ask his dad about that, too.

"Are you okay?" he asked.

"Yeah." She crossed her arms and began to rock. He sat beside her and rubbed her back.

"Do you think she's gone yet?" Herman asked after a while.

"Probably. It wouldn't have taken Hawkins long to get here in the speed boat."

They stood and she looked up at him. "Were the others planning to stay the night?"

"Yes."

"Let's go back then and be sociable. I want them to know I'm okay. We'll talk tonight?

"We'll talk all night if you want."

He stopped her on the landing and turned to face her.

"You were incredible tonight."

She shrugged. "I guess you never know what you're capable of until you're faced with an incredible situation."

As they walked back to the main house, Stephen, humbled by Herman's patience and understanding, realized he had found another reason to love her.

CHAPTER 33

Herman sat cross-legged on the bed facing Stephen in the soft light of a single lamp, with the north-facing wall of windows shut tight against the chilly night air. She could hear the deep rumble of a furnace from somewhere below. Stephen was naked but for his jeans, and Herman wore only his t-shirt; she tucked her hands between her legs to hold the shirt down and waited for him to open up. She wanted to know everything there was to know before she went to bed. She wanted the truth rather than Nina's version, and she wanted to hear it from him.

Slowly and not without shame, he explained to her how he was with Nina even the night they met.

"But, you had to be in love with someone to satisfy the curse," Herman said. "Surely, you weren't already in love with me?"

He nodded that he was. "From the first time I laid eyes on you. I've loved before, but I've never been *in* love. I knew the moment I saw you."

"But enough for the curse? You were *that* sure already?"

"Yes."

He told her about how different it was with Nina, physically. That he never let her touch him, and that to make sure she didn't, she never faced him when they had sex. "When they mated," was the way he put it, because, he said, it was no more romantic than two animals mating.

"So you never kissed her?" Herman asked.

"Only once, a long time ago. Just before I left to tour the States. That was when I took her virginity. I was drunk, and the whole thing was a mistake."

"Did you even have a girlfriend to feel unfaithful to at the time?"

"Not really. I left her in Japan."

"Your Japanese assistant?"

"Yes."

"Well, I can understand where Nina is coming from in a way, since you took my virginity too."

"It wouldn't have been any other way for Nina. She's been in love with me since we were kids. Knowing that we'd eventually make a baby together, she never had other boyfriends. She wasn't interested. She saved herself for me." Stephen lowered his eyes. "I took advantage of her emotionally. I wouldn't have done so physically. There's a fine line there, and I crossed it."

"You can't beat yourself up for the way she feels."

"You're defending me again, and I love you for it. But it's a moral dilemma I have to deal with, whether I'm responsible for the way she feels or not. I know I didn't make her fall in love with me. But I took advantage of it."

"But surely she must know that the curse wouldn't allow you to be a couple, even if you wanted to."

"That's not entirely true. If she is sterilized and there is no other way a purebred Curry can be born, she is free to do anything she wants. Once she's not my servant, she'll be my equal."

"Huh." Herman bit her nail, realizing as she did that it was a nervous habit she'd picked up from Stephen. "And you've explained to her that you two as a couple is not a possibility?"

"Of course. And I did everything I could to make sure she didn't misinterpret what we did to make the baby as intimacy. When we mated it lasted a minimal amount of time, we didn't speak, we didn't touch, and I left her right afterward."

"She said you brought her here and kept her naked. Why?"

"So she wouldn't feel equal to me at any point. I didn't enjoy seeing her that way, in fact I never looked at her unless I had to."

"And I guess you stayed on the island so you wouldn't get caught."

He raised an eyebrow in wry, silent acknowledgment. "I cast fertility spells all over the island, and on her and myself. I thought it would be my best chance to get it over and done with quickly."

"You must have come here when you told me you went to see my dad. Did you actually see him?"

"Yes, I did. I've never lied to you, Herman. I've only omitted to mention a few things."

"More than a few."

"I'm sorry."

Rather than allow her irritation to resurface, she pushed on. "When did you see my dad?"

"I ran into him at the airport as I was headed to Ottawa from New York. I looked for him there, but he'd canceled all his performances because you were missing. I went to North Carolina, too, all on the same day. On my return, I came straight to the island and stayed here for two days before I came home."

"And then you told me you loved me for the first time," Herman said.

Stephen nodded. "Nina lied to me after that. She knew she was pregnant, but she kept it from me. As soon as I suspected it, Margaret took her to the hospital for a blood test. Two days later, Nina told you."

"One other thing she said, I don't know if you heard it. She said you took her from her father and you were wed before nature, or something like that."

"She said that?"

"Yeah, the day you came home, I guess."

Stephen thought, and then realization dawned across his face.

"I left Hawkins at the boat and went back with Nina to get her case. I had a feeling that was when the baby was conceived, but I wasn't sure until now. I can see how her mind would warp it into something more romantic than it was."

"Was it on a screened-in porch like the one outside here?" She glanced toward the window where a door opened on a deck. Silhouetted against the moonlit trees outside was a sofa, which she assumed folded out into a bed. The bed from her dream. She felt sick.

"Yes. There's one on the far side of the other house. How did you know?"

"That was my nightmare."

"You dreamed about it?"

"Before it happened, yes. It was the night you left on your trip."

Herman wondered how she could have predicted such a thing, even unconsciously. It was too much to contemplate. She wrapped her arms around her body and rocked. She was glad he didn't reach out for her right then; she needed a moment to gather her nerves.

"So what now?" she asked eventually.

"I'll have to talk to her about her behavior, and I'm going to have to sympathize with her, to some extent. It's going to be like walking a tightrope."

It was Stephen's turn to go quiet. Before he spoke again, he took a deep breath in.

"Can I ask you a difficult question?"

She shrugged to show she wasn't bothered, which was a lie. "Why not?"

"What would you do if Nina lost the baby and I decided to make another one with her, to end the curse?"

Herman thought about it. It wouldn't be an ideal situation to have to go through it all again, by a far shot. But having decided she wanted to stay with him, and knowing she couldn't live with Nina hanging around, she made her choice. "I wouldn't be happy, of course, but I think I would understand. Just like I understand now that you had no choice, and that what you did with her is in no way equal to what we have."

A tear welled up in Herman's eye. She wiped it away and kissed him quickly, before she could change her mind. Longing rushed in with the warmth of his breath, with the need to keep him with her, beside her, inside her heart forever. She found she couldn't let go. She raised herself to her knees and wrapped her arms around his neck and kissed him until it was too uncomfortable to stay in the same position.

"Thank you," he murmured after their lips finally parted and she dropped back down on the bed.

"For what?"

"For making it so that I will never ever have to touch her again."

"How have I done that?"

"With your answer."

She frowned and waited for him to go on.

"When you said you would understand if I were to try to impregnate Nina again because you know it has nothing to do with our love, you made the curse null. I wouldn't feel as though I was being unfaithful to you, and so even though you and I have found love, and even if we are married, there is no point trying to impregnate Nina again. If I don't feel unfaithful, it wouldn't satisfy the curse anyway. Do you understand?"

"I think so."

"What it means is that if she doesn't have this baby, I can't undo the curse. The only circumstances that can are if she is sterilized, or if she dies childless while still in my employ. Otherwise, if she has children with another man, the curse passes down to our offspring, or Daphne's."

"You have to make sure she carries this baby to term," she said, thinking that if the whole situation wasn't over as soon as possible, she might be tempted to kill the girl herself. She knew better than to say what she was thinking; she'd seen the look in his eye earlier, and it unnerved her completely.

"At least I may be able to convince her that if she doesn't, she's not going to have another chance to conceive with me."

"Hopefully she'll want to hang on to the only thing she has left of you, then."

"It's not going to make her any easier to live with," he said cautiously.

"As long as you're with me, we'll deal."

She kissed him again. This time they didn't stop until they fell asleep in each other's arms.

***

At ten the next morning, Herman and Stephen emerged from their bedroom, ruffled, drowsy, and still pyjamaed, to find a fire crackling in the living room fireplace.

"There you guys are," Margaret said from the sofa. With her legs draped across Mark's lap and a coffee cup in hand, she looked cozy in an over-sized loose-knit sweater, a shade lighter of blue than the cardigan Herman wore over her nightshirt. "You missed Gerald. He had to go, but he insisted on not waking you up. Hawkins came to get him."

"I'll call him later," Stephen said. He turned to Herman. "Coffee, my love?"

"Yes, please."

"Here," Margaret said, holding out her cup to him. "You can top up mine, too."

"Mark?" Stephen asked.

The other man shook his scruffy blond head. "I'm good."

"You look like you haven't had much sleep," Margaret observed as Herman curled up in a ball on the opposite sofa.

"You're one to talk. I've never seen you looking quite so ... comfortable, before."

Margaret laughed. "We had fun last night."

Herman nodded once. "We were up most of the night talking."

"Are you okay?" Margaret asked gently, reminding Herman of the conversation they'd had on the phone the night Herman left.

"I'm better than I thought I'd be after seeing Nina for the first time. Am I okay? I'm not sure. It's a lot to swallow."

"Stephen's a good friend and all, but I don't know how you put up with it," Mark said.

Margaret answered for her. "True love can overcome circumstances that would destroy a relationship that was anything less." The look she gave him made Herman want to look away. She curled herself up tighter and closed her eyes. When she sensed Stephen had returned, she opened them to see Margaret sitting on Mark's lap, kissing him.

Stephen put Margaret's mug on the table in front of them and came to sit beside Herman. He handed her a cup of steaming black coffee. She took a deep whiff of it before taking a sip. He put his arm around her and she leaned back against him, hugging her cup.

"Do you want to go for a walk around the island before we go home?"

"So you can show me all the places you fucked Nina?" she murmured. She regretted saying it the second the words were out of her mouth.

"I can show you all the places I fucked Margaret too, if it'll make you feel better," he said just as quietly.

Herman sat up sharply and stared at him, shocked at what he had said. He shifted his gaze from Margaret to Herman, his expression impassive. "Does it really matter what I've done in the past and where, as long as I'm here with you in the present?"

Herman looked over at Margaret and Mark, who were still kissing and fondling one another. Stephen was right. What really mattered was now. The past couldn't be changed, and to live in it would be never to move forward.

"No," she said. "I'm sorry."

He kissed her hair without a word.

"I'd like to see the island with you," she said.

"Let's go in the kitchen and have breakfast first." He glanced at the other couple. "And leave these two to their mid-morning snack."

CHAPTER 34

Stephen kissed Herman goodbye and left her with Margaret and Mark at the boat launch on the mainland to drive to the house. It would have been faster for him to drive to the Curry residence to talk to Nina, or even to have ridden a horse, but he wanted the time to think about what he would say, and how he would say it. A storm was gathering; the smell of ozone, mingled with the sweet tang of lilacs, hung in the still, warm afternoon air. Stephen expected the rain would start within the hour.

He knocked at the Currys' front door and was surprised to see Lotta. Normally she worked at the house until dinnertime on Nina's day off. She explained apologetically that she had stayed home to care for Nina, who had spent the morning throwing up.

"I'm so afraid she'll get dehydrated, Sir," Lotta said. "I was just about to take some soup in to her. I'll let her know you're here."

"I can take it in and talk to her in her room—unless you think that would be inappropriate," he amended.

"Whatever you think best, Sir."

With a bowl of chicken noodle soup and crackers on a tray balanced on his left hand, Stephen rapped on Nina's bedroom door. Upon hearing a muffled, "Do I have to?" he announced himself.

"Master!" Nina said with a great amount of shuffling about. "Come in, please."

Disconcerted, but hardly surprised to see her room all

but wallpapered in posters of himself, he tried not to stare at the walls. She sat up in bed, dressed in an old-fashioned flannel nightie, and he placed the tray on her lap. He perched himself on the end of the bed and faced her. Nina stared at him with her mouth agape, as if unable to believe he was actually there in the flesh.

"We need to talk," he said. "But first, I want you to try to eat something."

At his command, she pulled herself together and picked up a cracker.

"Your mother tells me you were sick this morning."

"Yes, Master. I'm very sorry, Master. I promise I won't drink anymore." She bent her head and took a mouse-like nibble.

Stephen wholeheartedly wished he could tell Nina to stop with the "Master" crap for five minutes and simply talk to her, adult to adult, but to give her that equality even for a moment would upset the balance. Leading her to believe it could happen again while she was still bound to servitude would probably end in disaster. It might have worked for his father with Lotta, but the elder Curry was much more levelheaded than her romantically inclined, unbalanced daughter.

He watched her drink some of her soup, and when it looked like she might not run for the bathroom, he decided he may as well begin.

"I want to thank you, Nina."

Her eyes snapped open over the spoonful of soup she had just put to her lips. Stephen was glad she didn't have it in her mouth—he thought he might have worn it.

"You ... want to thank me?" She returned the spoon to the bowl slowly.

"Yes. You made me realize something. In fact, you made both myself and Miss Anderson realize something."

She stared at him, poised as though she was going to

take flight. He wondered if he had been hasty in thinking she was going to keep her lunch down. He decided to go on anyway.

"You showed us, inadvertently, that there is no longer any way I can feel unfaithful. Miss Anderson has accepted the conception of the baby and the reason behind why you and I had sex. So you see, if you were, God forbid, to lose this baby, there is no point in trying to conceive another one. The responsibility of the curse can no longer sit with me, because I would have to feel unfaithful, which I wouldn't."

"So, you're saying …"

"I'm saying the end of the curse rests entirely in your womb, Nina. If you have this baby, you can end it. Alternatively, if you have other children with someone else, then you will continue it. But now that I am with Miss Anderson, it is out of my hands."

Nina appeared to be in shock. He touched the lump under the blanket that he rightly assumed was her foot in an attempt to bring her back.

"Which is why it's so important for you to take care of yourself," he said, rubbing her foot. "Yourself and our baby."

She looked him in the eye. "Our baby," she repeated.

He felt suddenly, profoundly sorry for her.

"Oh, Master," she said, tears welling up in her eyes. "Nothing means more to me than our baby."

He moved the tray off her lap and sat closer to her. When he held out his arms, she fell into them. He wished he could take on some of the responsibility of looking after her while she carried his child. *His child,* he thought. But he couldn't see any way around the volatility of her feelings toward him.

Then it came to him. A way to make the baby real, with a single pronoun. "I know you can look after her then,"

Stephen said, rubbing her back.

"Her?" Nina released him quickly. "Do you really think it's a girl?" Tears ran down her cheeks and snot hung from her nose, and she looked at him as though he was Santa Claus.

"I get a strong sense that it is, yes." He had, in fact, known it was a girl from the moment he touched her and knew she was pregnant.

"A girl ..." she whispered, looking across the room into a distance she couldn't possibly be seeing. "Oh, Master, I hope it is a girl." She looked down at her belly and put her hand there, absentmindedly wiping her nose with her other sleeve.

"I promise," she said, looking into his eyes with renewed determination. "I promise I will look after her, after the both of us. After your daughter." She smiled at him, and he took both of her hands in his when it seemed she was going to kiss him.

"Thank you, Nina," he said sincerely.

He left her eating her lunch with the hope that she would behave herself for the rest of the pregnancy.

***

The downpour started with large, heavy drops and escalated to a driving rain within seconds. Stephen reveled in the sensation of frigid water running down his scalp, dripping off his hair and down the back of his neck, running in a stream down his body, making his clothes heavy and his toes swim, each in their own pool that were his shoes. It made him feel alive. It made him think of all the things he wanted to share with his daughter when she was old enough. Wrapped up in Nina's emotions and the drama that surrounded the pregnancy, he hadn't given the baby herself much heed. He had registered the concept of being a father without considering the wealth of potential a new child held. To create life was awe-inspiring. He saw that life in Nina when he sat down and spoke to her calmly, without any of the stress that had inundated every encounter with her previously. His new revelation also made him realize that it was fortunate he and Herman would be on the road for much of the time during the pregnancy. The desire to feel the baby move inside her excited him; he was anxious to feel the realness and the individuality of the being he had helped to create. The lack of emotion that went into the making of the baby was equal and opposite to the protectiveness he felt for her now; it rivaled any emotion he'd ever encountered, and he wasn't sure he trusted himself to stay far away from the baby if he didn't have to.

Arriving home, he stepped through the front door and stood with his back to it, dripping on the inside mat. Herman sat on the stairs, her elbows on her knees. They stared silently at each other for a full minute before she rose and came to him. She wrapped her arms around his neck without hesitation over his sopping clothes and stretched to press up against him and kiss him deeply. As he embraced her, he allowed himself to escape from his myriad of thoughts into the sensation of her lips and her warm body.

"How did it go?" she asked when their lips parted.

He shrugged. "It went."

"We can go on with our lives now?"

"Yes." Herman lowered her head but Stephen wasn't willing to let thoughts of Nina interfere. "What is it?" he asked.

"'I did a lot of thinking while I waited for you to get back." She tipped her chin up and her blue eyes gazed into his. "Three weeks ago, for the first time in my life I stepped out on my own. Since then, I've been through the worst day of my life and now I'm here. With you."

"Herman, I ..."

She put her fingers to his lips and quieted him. "I might

not be the happiest I'll ever be right now, but I have lots of hope for us. As long as we're together, I've got to believe we can do anything. Because we're connected by something way beyond what the rest of the world sees." She placed her hands on his cheeks. "Does that sound about right to you?"

"Yes. I know what we have is magic. And we'll make it through this and whatever else life throws at us."

"Make love to me, Stephen."

He kissed her. "I love you."

They walked hand in hand to the bath room, Stephen leaving a trail of soggy footprints.

epilogue

The day before they were to leave Kingston and go out on tour, Stephen received a call from Gerald to say that he was needed at the old lawyer's house right away. Gerald refused to say what it was about on the phone. Stephen left Herman at the station to oversee the crew, who were about to leave with a tractor-trailer full of equipment and props, and drove to Gerald's house.

"What's all the secrecy?" he asked Gerald when the old man opened the door and welcomed him into his manse in person.

"It's not so much a matter of secrecy, my boy. It's time-sensitive, as they say these days."

They walked through the high-ceilinged foyer where Stephen had played hide-and-seek with Gerald's grandchildren, and to the back of the house, into the forbidden library of his childhood. The room was dominated by a bulky oak desk, which held a computer with a large screen. On the screen, Stephen was shocked to see a man he resembled closely.

"Dad!"

"Hello, Stephen." His father smiled. The two years since he had seen his father in person hadn't changed him, but for a single white streak in his hair, over his left eye. In the background, Stephen recognized the living room of the house in Antigua; they had visited the family estate every winter until his parents and sister moved there permanently.

"Gerald tells me we need to talk," Tarmien Dagmar said to his son.

"I'll leave you two alone then, shall I?" Gerald grinned and backed out of the room.

"You look surprised to see me. I assume that's Gerald, meddling again."

"That's one way to put it." Stephen laughed, grateful to the old man for ending his procrastination by force. "How are you? I haven't heard from you lately."

"Fine, fine. Your mother is busy with charities, and Daphne's social life takes up most of her time. I'm trying not to enjoy semi-retirement too much, lest your mother start getting me involved. She's already hinting."

"What about you? I hear you're about to start touring again."

"I am. We leave tomorrow, in fact."

"And how about your new assistant, Herman. Have you made any decisions?"

"I've gone one step further." He lowered his eyes, knowing Tarmien could see his face. They had never discussed, as adults, his dad's forced affair with Lotta and what it did to Stephen's mother. Stephen's avoidance of him for months after he saw how his mom had reacted to finding that her husband had had a child with his servant, showed Tarmien how his son felt about the betrayal. What they *had* discussed was how Stephen planned to carry out the requirement of the curse; Tarmien had urged him to do it before he married rather than after.

"You really love this girl then," Tarmien said.

"I do. And you have a grandchild on the way. Nina is pregnant already."

A gasp came from behind Tarmien, and he turned to the sound. "Stella ..."

"Mom?" Stephen's stomach knotted. "I'm sorry," he called, though he couldn't see her. He watched his father get up and leave the frame of the screen and he waited. A few minutes later, both his parents appeared. His mother sat and his father stood behind her with his hand on her shoulder.

"I'm sorry, Mom," Stephen repeated.

He saw her shake her head, more to herself than to negate his apology. "It had to be done, Stephen. Hopefully we can be free of this horrible plague over your father's family."

He noted that she didn't include herself, and that hurt as much as the pain of putting her through the reminder of her husband's infidelity.

"How are you?" she asked.

"I'm doing well. Herman and I are very happy together."

Stella Dagmar hesitated, her mouth open, apparently willing herself to speak.

"Does she know about the baby?"

"Yes, she does. And she understands it was the curse that made me do it."

His mother's eyes filled with tears. "And she's forgiven you?"

"She has."

"You've found yourself a wonderful girl, then. Don't mess it up."

"I won't," Stephen said as his mother got up and left. Tarmien sat down in her place.

"Will she forgive me, do you think?" he asked his father after a moment passed.

"She doesn't blame you, Stephen. She'll be okay. I'll look after her."

"Before you go, can I ask you something?"

"What's that?"

"I know Nina's baby is a girl. Is that one of our gifts?" The question had been plaguing Stephen since he realized

244

he knew, in his heart, the sex of the baby.

A slight twinge lowered his father's brow. "I knew from the moment you and Daphne were conceived that your mother was pregnant and what your genders were. Your grandfather didn't tell me about that part of our magic, so I wondered if it would be passed on to you." Tarmien rubbed his chin and his frown deepened. "We need to talk, Stephen."

"It sounds serious."

"I think it can wait until the baby is born. How is Nina handling her pregnancy so far? When is she due?"

"I calculated late December. She's fine physically ..."

"And emotionally?"

"She thinks she's in love with me."

"But she'll have a hysterectomy when it's all done?"

"Only because she thinks we can be together after that."

"I see." His father nodded. "I'm going to talk to Gerald about getting a Power of Attorney made up so that, should she suffer any sort of mental breakdown, Lotta can make her medical decisions for her. And in the meantime, you're making yourself scarce, yes?"

"The tour will take me away most of the time until after my daughter is born."

His dad shook his head. "My baby's having a baby. It's hard to believe."

Just as Stephen opened his mouth to ask his father about the redness in his eyes during the incident on the island, the older man interrupted him.

"I really have to go and talk to your mother. Try to come to Antigua, will you? If you have a break? We'd love to meet Herman."

"I'll do my best. Take care, Dad."

"And you. We love you, Stephen."

"Love you too, Dad. And Mom, too."

"I'll tell her."

***

He expected to find Herman at the house by the time he returned. After gaining confirmation from Hawkins that she hadn't come back from the station, he ran out to the barn, bridled a mare, and galloped out.

"The crew left half an hour ago," she said when he stepped in the door and found her sitting in the old waiting room. "I was enjoying the quiet.

"What ...?" She looked puzzled at his expression, and it was no wonder. He was puzzled about the way he felt. He had just told his parents to expect their first grandchild, yet the circumstances were wrong. He stood facing the woman that he wanted to spend the rest of his life with, the woman he loved more than life itself, but she wasn't the one pregnant with his child.

He walked to the bench and sat beside her, and she relaxed against his body.

"You looking forward to the change of scenery?" he asked.

"I'm looking forward to seeing Chad again, more than anything."

"That's why I arranged to make Ottawa our first stop on the tour."

"He's going to love you." She sighed and snuggled her face against his chest. "All I really want is to be a family."

"Believe me," Stephen said as he lifted her chin and looked into her eyes, "there's nothing more I want in the world."

ACKNowledgments

I'd like to thank my scads of beta readers, all of whom helped immensely to enhance my story. They are, in order of when they read it from earliest to latest: Jeanine Lebsack; Janice Hillgren; my foodie friend who helped me lay the Dagmar's table, Jolene Mottern; Deborah Cousins; Deborah Drucker; Pamela Read; Paul R. Davis; Megan Starkweather; cover artist extraordinaire, Belinda Borradaile; and the girls from the Old-School Romance Book Club: Cathy Akridge; Marielena Browne; Kristi Hannan; Linda Upton; Violet Olivo; Whitney Butler; Beth Hale; Syeda Faiza Rasheed; and my friend and fellow language-lover, Milly Bellegris. Thanks also to Patricia Brown for the wonderful editing advice, Brandi Woolard for her expert opinion on things witchy, and Rylan Schwarze—Rynestone, magician with an edge—who gave me insight on the life, practice, and business that is magic on the road. Any inaccuracies in this book are on me. Special thanks to my best friend and literary sounding board, John Vandenberg.

Many thanks to the City of Kingston for its inspiration. While most of the places mentioned in this book are fictitious, these are some special points of interest: the Hochelaga Inn, which is the inspiration for the Dagmar house (book a night in the tower room!); K-Rock 105.7; Kingston's Grand Trunk Railway station, which I resurrected as a nightclub for the purpose of my story; and the Kingston airport, whose land I expropriated for the locale of the Dagmar house. The walk back to town was lovely.

I want to take this opportunity to thank my living muse, Sakurai Atsushi. Your lyrics, your stage presence, and your fashion sense rock my world. My profound thanks go to the music of Buck-Tick; my momentum exists in the rhythm of your songs.

Finally, thank you—yes, you!—for reading my book. For updates on the release of *The Great Dagmaru – Book 2*, please visit my blog at lindaghill.com and sign up for my mailing list (coming soon). And please remember to leave a review of this book! Even a few words are greatly appreciated.

Cheers!

Linda

ABOUT THE AUTHOR

Linda G. Hill was born and raised an only child in Southern Ontario, Canada. She credits the time she spent alone when she was growing up, reading books and building worlds and characters of her own to keep her company, as the reason she became a writer.

A stay-at-home mom of three beautiful boys, Linda is a graduate of the Writing Program at St. Lawrence College in Brockville, Ontario. Aside from caring for her family, she enjoys traveling the world, eating trout cooked on the barbecue, and of course, reading.